Johnny Ste

Tracks in the Snow

Joel Schnoor

Gennesaret Press

Gennesaret Press
202 Persimmon Place
Apex, NC 27523

www.GennesaretPress.com

© 2016 Joel Schnoor. All rights reserved.

No part of this book may be reproduced or transmitted by
any means without the express written consent of the author.

ISBN: 978-0-9845541-6-4

Library of Congress Control Number: 2015914006

Printed in the United States of America
Apex, North Carolina

Cover design by Nathan Schnoor
Illustrations by Subrata Dutta & Dipali Dutta

To my wife Michelle

Who is my encourager, my chief editor, my accountability partner, my motivator, my sounding board, and the love of my life.

Thank you, Michelle. This project could not have happened without you.

Table of Contents

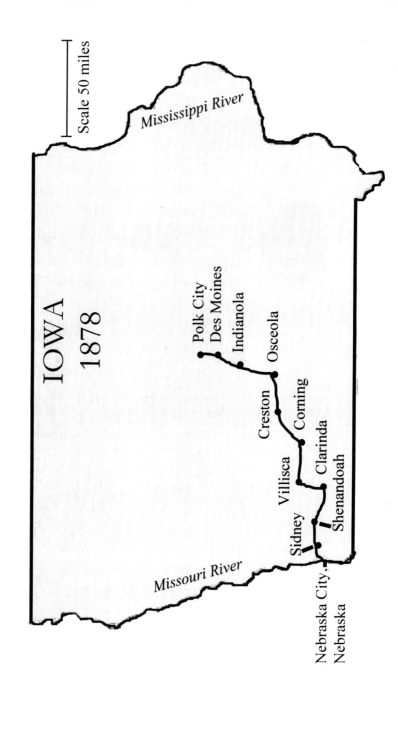

Scale 50 miles

Mississippi River

IOWA
1878

Polk City
Des Moines
Indianola
Osceola
Creston
Corning
Clarinda
Villisca
Shenandoah
Sidney
Nebraska City,
Nebraska

Missouri River

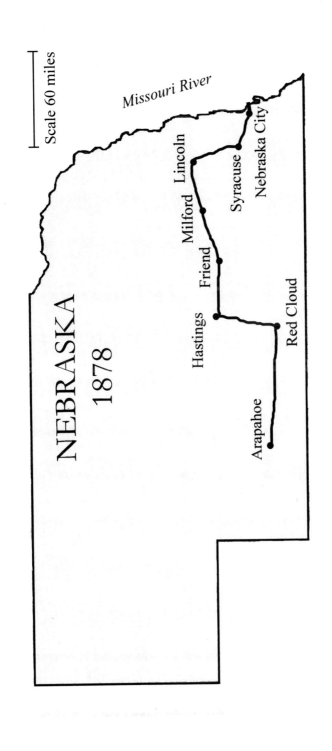

Scale 60 miles

Missouri River

Lincoln
Milford
Friend
Hastings
Syracuse
Nebraska City
Red Cloud
Arapahoe

NEBRASKA
1878

1

Doc Hubbard's House

Early February, 1878

Kate, do you realize that you are sitting in the same chair that a dead man sat in just a month ago?" Kate glanced up from the book she had been reading—one of Doc Hubbard's books. She was sitting in Doc Hubbard's chair, behind Doc Hubbard's desk, in Doc Hubbard's study, which was in Doc Hubbard's house.

The howling, brutally cold wind rattled the shutters and whistled through the rafters. The creaks and groans of the old house, magnified with the darkness of a heavy snowfall, seemed ominous, almost sinister.

"Well, he wasn't dead when he sat in it, and it's not like he is still here, wanting to sit in his chair, is it?"

"I am not so sure about that," I replied, trying hard to sound eerie.

"What do you mean?" asked Kate. "He can't be here … can he?"

"He might be," I suggested.

"No, he can't be … I think," said Kate, not quite convinced.

"I may be able to prove it," I said.

"How?"

"Well, every time you sit in that chair, you look a little more like old Doc Hubbard."

"Do not."

"Do too!" I said. "You look a little older; your hair gets a little grayer; and you get wrinkles in your forehead. Look in this mirror. Tell me what you see." I tilted the slate board up so that she could look at it.

"Oh my! That does look like Doc Hubbard!" gasped Kate.

I laughed, happy that she recognized the person in my drawing.

Kate giggled. "Johnny, you're silly," she said.

"You are certainly right about that," said Ma, sticking her head in the door. "Go wash up, children. It's almost time to eat, but I need a little help from each of you first."

The tantalizing smells of cornbread and Ma's beef stew found their way into the room, and Kate and I didn't need to be told twice.

After cleaning our hands in the wash bowl and helping Ma put the food on the table, we sat down. It wasn't our table; it was Doc Hubbard's table. Well, it wasn't really his either, because he was dead, but it had been his table.

We were there—in Doc Hubbard's house, that is— on account of our house burning down about a month before, in December, right after the Christmas pageant at school. About the same time that we lost the house, Doc Hubbard died in a train wreck in Ashtabula, Ohio, on his way back from a trip east.

Doc Hubbard's daughter, his heir—she lived in Boston—sent a letter to Sheriff Cogswell saying that she would not be able to come out to our town of Polk City,

Iowa until sometime in the spring, and she asked the sheriff to arrange for a "reputable family" to stay in the house as a sort of caretaker.

For the first few days right after the fire, we had stayed with our neighbors the next farm over. Squeezing all of us into the Hudson's house was tough—Pa said it was like trying to stuff two coyotes into one sheepskin, and that if we wanted to remain friends with the Hudsons then we should stay in a different house. He was probably right.

The sheriff knew that we needed a place to stay. He apparently figured that our family was as reputable as any, because he said we were the logical choice to live in the house.

Doc Hubbard's house was spacious—it certainly had more room (and more rooms) than we were used to. Kate and I enjoyed exploring the rooms, especially the attic, where Doc had kept several boxes of books and artifacts from his travels.

It was a nice house—not opulent, but comfortable and well-furnished—and it had everything we needed. We had lost just about everything in the fire except for the shirts on our backs and a few odds and ends, like the kitchen oven, that didn't burn in the flames. The house certainly did not lack for chairs, beds, blankets, and those kinds of daily comforts that we sometimes take for granted.

Ma said grace to bless the meal, and then the three of us began eating. The others—Pa, and my brothers George, Elias, and Ott—were out at the farm all day, fixing up the two wagons that we would be taking on our trip west.

Except for the horses—Millie and Billy—we kept the animals at the farm because, fortunately, our barn hadn't burned down in the fire. Besides, Doc Hubbard didn't have a barn. He was a doctor, not a farmer. The two horses were stabled in town at a nearby livery.

Doc's house was about three miles from the farm. Pa hired my best friend Sam Hudson to help look after the animals, even though Pa went out to the farm most everyday.

"Ma?" asked Kate.

"Yes, Kate?"

"Do we really have to move?"

"I thought you wanted to move," said Ma, "and the answer is yes."

"But why?" asked Kate. "We like this house."

"I think you know why," Ma said softly. "And besides, this isn't our house."

"I know, I know, we're going so we can get a place of our own in Kansas or Nebraska, where it isn't so crowded. But Ma, I'll miss my friends, especially Nellie and Madee and Sam and Clarence."

"Kate, you will make new friends wherever we end up."

After we cleaned up the kitchen, Ma told Kate and me to clean Dr. Hubbard's study. Without hesitation, Kate and I ran into the room, closed the door, and grabbed the two feather dusters that were on the floor, behind the desk, where we had put them the last time we "cleaned" the study.

"You can be Doc Rooster first," squealed Kate as quietly as a person can squeal but still have it be a whisper.

I took a feather duster in each hand, jumped behind the davenport—a kind of a bench with a soft cushion to sit on—and began clucking and strutting like a rooster. Kate retrieved the balls—three of Doc Hubbard's socks, each rolled up and tied with string into a bundle—from the top drawer of the desk and took her position across the room. As I danced back and forth, she took aim and threw the balls at me, one at a time. If she hit me on a throw, she got a point. If she missed on all three throws, then I got a point. Then we traded places.

The score was fifteen to fourteen when we heard Ma humming just outside the door. A few seconds later, the door opened, and Ma found us busily working on cleaning.

"Kate, you are talented to be able to use two feather dusters at once," said Ma.

"It … um … it goes faster than just using one," said

Kate. "See? The bookcase is almost clean."

"I see," said Ma, nodding. "Johnny, how does the room look on your side?"

"It looks good, Ma, from over here. Wait—Kate, I see a speck of dust on Ludwig van."

Kate brushed the feather duster over the small bust of Beethoven on the bookcase.

"That's better," I said. "I think we're almost done."

"I'll give you a few more minutes to finish up in here," said Ma, "but then I'm going to need your help on other tasks."

"Yes, ma'am," we said in unison, looking at each other.

"What's the score?" asked Ma.

"Fifteen to—" began Kate, before covering her mouth with her hands. She blushed.

"Now children, do finish up," said Ma, with a hint of a smile.

Later in the afternoon, the front door flew open and in marched Pa and my brothers, Ott, Elias, and George. They closed the door and then removed their coats, hanging them on a coat rack that was next to the door. Before coming in, they had brushed most of the snow off of their coats but they hadn't cleaned their boots yet, which they then did, in turn, with an old towel that had been hanging on the coat rack for that very purpose. After having lived for a month in that house, we all had been trained and were prepared to pass Ma's rigorous inspections.

"Hot cider, anyone?" asked Ma.

"Yes, please!" cried Ott. "Anything hot, really, would be wonderful. It's cold out there."

"The last of our cider from the barrel is warming on the stove," said Ma. "It should be ready now."

"How are the animals, Pa?" asked Kate, as we made our way to the table.

"The animals are all fine, and they were asking about you," said Ott.

"Asking about me?" asked Kate, smiling.

"Yes, of course," said Elias. "Henry VIII was cock-a-doodling something that sounded just like, 'Where's the girl now, where's the girl now?'"

"And Ollie was oinking something that could have been, 'Kate Kate Katee, Kate Kate Kateeeee!'" said George, with a twinkle in his eye.

Pa said, "And the real clincher was when the sheep started singing, 'Ka-aa-aa-ate, Ka-aa-aa-ate.'"

"Did the sheep really say … hey wait a minute, we don't have any sheep!" she exclaimed.

We all, including Kate, burst into laughter.

2
Who Is Thunder

The shiny black coat of my stallion Thunder glistened in the setting sun as we stood on the ridge overlooking the valley below. A gentle westerly breeze brushed against my face, running invisible fingers across the whisker stubble on my chin. The evening sky exuded serenity, but I knew the evening would be anything but peaceful. My eyes focused on the ridge opposite me across the valley. I was waiting for Indians.

Apache, Sioux, Otoe, Ute, Blackfoot, and Cherokee—any or all would be appearing soon. How many? I didn't know. All I knew was that the good citizens of the town depended on me for their survival, though they didn't realize it. And as long as I could preserve my anonymity, I would be relatively free to continue defending the new communities springing up in the American West.

My scout spies—George, Elias, and Ott—had done excellent work, as always, in discovering the planned attack on Nebraskaville, and, as always, they volunteered to help prevent the attack from succeeding.

They knew, though, that Thunder and I rode with superior speed, and they also realized that my sharpshooting skills were *nonpareil*. No one could shoot with my accuracy. No, this was something I had to do alone.

Then I saw it. My eagle eyes detected a single feather rising up from behind a rock on the ridge across the valley. Then I saw another. And then another. Before long, I counted roughly one hundred Indian warriors standing opposite me. I don't think they saw me—I don't even think they were looking for me.

They had strength in numbers. I, however, had the element of surprise. They were expecting to raid the town unopposed. They had another thing coming.

A cacophony of war whoops erupted, and the Indian horde began streaming down the ridge. It was time to make my move.

Because of the cliffs bordering most of the western edge of Nebraskaville, I knew that the warriors would have to go through Broken Bow Pass. Thunder and I raced down the back side of the ridge and flew toward the pass.

I stopped about a hundred yards this side of the pass at a little-known crevice that provided an entry way through the ridge into the valley, dismounted quickly, and took position behind a cluster of boulders that gave me both the perfect view and the optimal shooting angle.

The sun had set by then, but fortunately a full moon provided all the light I needed. As the first wave of warriors came through the pass, I began firing my Winchester repeating rifle. I didn't hit any Indians—I wasn't aiming at them. My bullets hit and ricocheted off the obsidian boulder protruding from the rock wall behind the pass entrance. I had researched the geology of the area earlier that afternoon and, though most of the rock face was limestone, a small obsidian outcropping made itself particularly convenient for me. The bullets that normally

would sink into limestone bounced cleanly off the harder obsidian.

The ricochets gave the illusion that there were more guns shooting at the Indians than there really were. Many of the attackers halted their advance, confused and probably trying to determine what to do next. Some of them kept on coming though, apparently able to see through my ruse. With loud, blood-curdling screams, they began closing in on me. Little did they know that I had foreseen this and had prepared for this possibility.

Quickly, I reached into the brush and pulled out the Gatling gun I had hidden earlier in the day, and I opened fire just over their heads. The spray of bullets mowed off most of the feathers they were wearing.

They turned tail and ran.

"We got 'em, Thunder!" I cried. "We stopped them!"

Thunder turned to me and nuzzled my shoulder. Then he pushed against my shoulder.

"What is it, Thunder? What's the matter?" I mumbled.

Thunder … or something … pushed hard against my shoulder again.

"Who is Thunder?" a voice called out.

"What?"

"Who is Thunder? You said something like, 'What is it, Thunder?'"

I opened an eye. I saw Ott.

"I think you were having a dream," he said.

"I … I don't know."

"What was it about?"

"Thunder and I … saved the town. We stopped them."

"Stopped who?"

"Them. The warriors … the attacking Indians."

I opened both eyes. My brother Ott, propped up on one elbow, was next to me in bed.

"I think someone's excited about moving west," said Ott.

"I guess so. Yeah, I think so."

I fell back asleep, not waking up again until it was time to get up for breakfast.

"Go get your Pa for breakfast, Johnny. He's in the study," said Ma.

I staggered into the study, still groggy from sleep and perhaps feeling exhausted from spending the night saving Nebraskaville from the attacking Indians.

"Mornin', Pa," I yawned. "It's time to eat."

He was sitting at Doc Hubbard's desk, studying something.

"What are you looking at?" I asked.

"Maps," said Pa.

"Maps!" Now I was awake. Maps interested me. "Is this for the trip?"

"Exactly. I bought these the other day at Ledbetter's." Ledbetter's was the general store in town.

"Have you figured out a route west?"

"I believe I have!" Pa's voice somehow sounded younger than it had for a long time. It sounded stronger. "Of course, it's always subject to change, but at least we will have a starting plan."

"Can you show me?" I asked.

"Of course," said Pa. "Here's about where Polk City is, right in the middle of Iowa. And here's where we're hoping to end up, somewhere near the middle of Nebraska. We'll head to Red Cloud, Nebraska, where we may stay with the Cockralls—your Uncle Frank and Aunt Rachel Anne, my sister—while we look for some land where we can make a homestead claim."

Pa spoke with excitement in his voice. I looked up at him and his eyes were shining, kind of like looking into someone's eyes when he's watching fireworks in the night sky.

"I can't wait to get started on the trip, Pa."

"Me too, Johnny. Me too."

3
Knocking on the Door

You know how, when you're in the store and you see a new toy or a new book or a new kind of candy sitting on the shelf, you find yourself thinking, "If I only could have that new thing, wouldn't life be grand?"

Well, I reckon that adults think that way about moving to new places. At least, after word got out that we were soon to head west, it seemed half the people in town decided they wanted to come along with us. It wasn't like a plague was sweeping through town or that gold had been discovered on the plains of Nebraska. People just appeared to be itchin' to move on and live somewhere different.

One morning, only a few days before we were planning to leave Polk City, we were about halfway through breakfast—a stack of hotcakes and sorghum molasses—when a rapid knocking on the front door startled me.

Knock! Knock! Knock!

Ma got up out of her chair and walked toward the door. Before she reached it, the knocking occurred again.

Knock! Knock! Knock!

The door opened and the plump head of a woman, perhaps thirty years old with a mound of curly blond hair,
appeared in the opening.

"Halloo!" she called out in a shrill voice. "Anyone—"

"Hello, Miss—" said Ma.

"Pardon me, Mrs. Stevens, I apologize for just barging
in like this. When no one answered, I thought you may
not have heard my—"

"It's quite all right," said Ma. "Do come in, please."

The woman stepped into the house. I recognized her as
the lady who worked in the town bakery. Pa bought me a
doughnut from her once, so I had fond memories of her.

"Let me start over," said the woman. "Ahem. Well, hello,
Mrs. Stevens. I am Lucille O'Neill—you may know me
from the bakery—and I am here to inquire as to whether
you indeed have room available on your journey west."

"Well, I don't believe that we're looking to add anyone
to the party," said Ma hesitantly, "and if—"

"Oh Mrs. Stevens, I wouldn't be any trouble a'tall. I can
cook and clean and pack and carry and sew and chop and
start campfires and wash and sing and nurse and skin a
rabbit and deliver a foal and milk a cow and tan a hide
and pickle the cucumbers and churn the butter and shoot
the left wing off a June bug from a hundred yards away—"

"Miss O'Neill," interrupted Ma, "can you—"

"Left-handed," continued Miss O'Neill, finishing her
sentence.

Ma stood there with a sort of dazed expression, as if
she had just been hit in the head with a big stick and was

trying to remember who she was, but she quickly gathered herself.

"Please, Miss O'Neill, tell me, why are you interested in going out west?"

"Well, you see," said Miss O'Neill, gasping to catch her breath, "my sister lives in McCook, Nebraska—she moved out there about a year ago … well, no, actually it was more like two years ago … two? No, I think it was perhaps five years ago … I'm not sure. Let's see, it was right after Aunt Mildred eloped with that snake oil salesman from Biloxi, which was in … oh, it was after the war … well of course it was after the war, because Sadie hadn't even been born yet, and—"

"Ahem," interrupted Ma, "Miss O'Neill, I think that—"

"Well, to make a long story short," said Miss O'Neill, "I have recently been informed that my sister Gertrude has been taken ill with the palsy. I want to head out to McCook to see what I can do to help, and perhaps I can assist her and her husband in moving back east where there is more medical help available. After all, Gertrude's husband Jack is a nice fellow and supposedly a good accountant, but he's not of much use in the practical things of life."

"That all sounds very reasonable, Miss O'Neill, but I do believe our wagon party is full. We have two wagons to carry seven people," said Ma.

"I certainly do understand, Mrs. Stevens," Miss O'Neill replied. "If you somehow have space open up—perhaps you'll have an additional wagon that could use another person—then please let me know. I am quite certain that I want to—need to, even—end up in McCook, Nebraska sometime this spring. Why, I'll even walk to McCook if there's no other way."

Ma smiled. "We will certainly keep you in mind, Miss O'Neill, should anything become available. We don't want you to have to walk all the way to McCook now, do we?"

Miss O'Neill hadn't been gone for more than ten minutes before we had another knock at the door.

Knock! Knock! Knock!

Pa opened the door and standing there was Sheriff Cogswell.

"Morning, John."

"Morning, Sheriff."

"John, I received a telegram from Doc Hubbard's daughter. She asked if you were interested in buying any of the furniture. She plans to sell everything when she comes out here, but she wanted to give you the first crack at it. She also wanted to know when you thought you'd be heading out. Are you still looking at Monday?"

"Yes sir," said Pa, "I think Monday it is. Thank her for her generosity. I'll talk with Catherine and we'll decide if we want to take the furniture. Sometimes traveling light is easier."

"Oh, by the way," said the sheriff, "I have a brother out in Friend, Nebraska. If you pass that way, stop in and say howdy. He's a good guy."

"I don't doubt that, Sheriff. If he's kin to you, he's bound to be a good guy."

"Take care, John, and God-speed on your trip."

They shook hands and the sheriff left.

And maybe fifteen minutes after Sheriff Cogswell left, there was someone at the door again.

Knock! Knock! Knock!

Pa answered the door only to find Mr. Dinwidden standing there. He was looking down at the ground, like he was studying his shoes. He glanced up for a moment but then looked back down. He cleared his throat and then spoke.

"Hello, Mr. Stevens … uh … John. I want to talk to you about something but wish to do so in private."

"Sure, Gene," said Pa. He stepped outside and closed the door.

The rest of us ate in silence at first, not out of politeness or reverence so much as just wanting to eavesdrop on the conversation. All I could hear were muffled voices. I couldn't make out any distinct words.

Finally, Kate asked the question we were all thinking: What are they talking about?

"Johnny, you haven't been picking on Eugene recently, have you?" asked Ma.

Ma was referring to Eugene Dinwidden III, the spoiled brat of a boy who was in our one-room schoolhouse and was the proverbially constant thorn in my side.

"No, I haven't, Ma," I said. "Kate, have you beaten up Eugene lately?"

"How long ago is lately? I haven't touched him for well over a week," said Kate, with a somewhat devious smile.

"Well, I know one thing," I said. "There are a lot of things about Polk City that I'm going to miss, but I'm sure not going to miss Eugene Dinwidden III. That boy just drives me nuts. He's got about as much sense as a possum that fell out of a tree and landed on his head."

Ma frowned. "Johnny, you know better than to say that."

"It's true, though, Ma," argued Kate. "In fact, I think the best thing about moving from Polk City is that we get away from that awful Eugene."

"Children, please," said Ma. "God made Eugene just like he made you and me, and God loves Eugene just as much as he loves you and me. You might not like the things Eugene says or does, but he is a neighbor and deserves to be loved by us, just like any other neighbor. Isn't that right?"

I looked at Kate and she looked at me. I could feel my face turning red. Kate's certainly was.

"Yes ma'am," I replied. "You're right, Ma. I'm sorry."

"I'm sorry too, Ma," said Kate.

After a few more minutes of silence, the door opened and Pa stepped back inside, closing the door behind him.

Pa had a smile on his face.

"What happened, Pa?" asked Elias.

"The Lord works in mysterious ways," said Pa.

"What do you mean?" asked Ott.

"Let's put it this way. We try to set our own plans; we get ideas fixed in our minds as to how life should be. We think we're in charge of the whole shootin' match, and then …"

"And then what, Pa?" asked George.

"And then God turns things upside down and reminds us that it's his plan we should be following, not our own."

"John, you're teasing the kids," said Ma. "What happened?"

Pa grinned. "The Dinwiddens are joining us on our trip west."

4
Wagons West

O tt, you awake?" I whispered. It was Sunday night, February 10, 1878, mere hours before we were to set out for our new home across the plains. I was having trouble falling asleep. We had stayed up very late that night packing the wagons, trying to get everything ready so that in the morning we could quickly load up and go, but there was still work to do. Feelings of anxiety and frustration were haunting me, and I wanted to talk to Ott. Trouble was, Ott was a heavy sleeper. Pa said that Ott slept so deeply that a steam locomotive could run right through our house and it wouldn't even wake Ott.

I shook him. "Ott? Are you awake?" I repeated.

I heard a voice whisper next to me. "No, you're talking to somebody who looks like Ott, acts like Ott, sounds like Ott, and is almost as funny as Ott, but Ott is fast asleep and, if you know what's good for you, you'll soon be asleep, too. Otherwise, you might make someone's youngest older brother quite irate."

"Huh?" I shrugged, confused.

"What I'm saying is this: I'm tired and want to go to sleep, and I suggest you do the same. Tomorrow is going to be a long, busy day."

"I suppose you're right, Ott. It's just that … I'm kinda mad that Pa invited the Dinwiddens to go with us out to Nebraska. I don't know what possessed Pa to say yes. I was looking forward to this trip like an adventure, something fun and exciting. Now I'm feeling all anxious, and my stomach is in knots. I don't know why. It's not fear … I don't know what it is. Maybe it's dread."

"Maybe, or maybe it's the anticipation of uncertainty," said Elias from across the room.

"Uncertainty?" asked George, who was also now awake. "You mean like the uncertainty of being able to get sweet little Lillian Steinmetz to smile at you?"

THUMP!

I couldn't tell for sure in the dark, but I suspected that George had just been hit in the head with a pillow. A hushed laugh came from Elias.

"For what it's worth," said George, "I'm a little nervous too. New places, new faces, new routines, new everything—this whole move will be a new experience for all of us. It will be an adventure, with or without Eugene. That's for certain. Why did Pa invite the Dinwiddens? I don't know, but Pa must know what he's doing."

"The thing I like to think about," said Elias, "is the story of Joshua, when he was about to lead the people of Israel into the promised land. God told him several times to be strong, to be courageous. God said he would stay with Joshua, and he did. That helps me."

"Me too," said Ott.

"Good night, guys," I said, closing my eyes, "and thanks." I felt much better and I think I fell asleep not long after.

Morning—and the ensuing chaos of finishing our packing, cleaning, and making sure we didn't forget anything—came all too quickly, but as the first rays of sunlight reached their fingers over the horizon, revealing clear, deep blue skies, the morning promised to be a pretty one. George and Elias hitched up the horses to the wagons, and finally, shortly after eight o'clock, we were ready to go.

"Giddup," said Pa, almost matter-of-factly, and the frozen ground crackled under the wheels as the first wagon lurched into motion. The second and third wagons followed as our little train of three wagons began its journey across the plains. We were Nebraska-bound!

Ma and Pa were in the first wagon, and Kate and I were walking alongside.

In the second wagon sat Mr. and Mrs. Dinwidden, Eugene, and Miss O'Neill, who had somehow managed to talk the Dinwiddens into letting her join them.

In the third wagon, George held the reins and Elias and Ott were walking.

Old Jack, my yellow dog and trustworthy companion, trotted along under the lead wagon. He took it upon himself to be the protector and defender of our little traveling party. Pa said that an alert watchdog could help make sure that valuable family property—especially the horses—didn't disappear in the middle of the night. I was glad that Old Jack was with us.

I found out later that we were carrying some freight of value. It wasn't the stoves, nor was it anything else that we had salvaged from the fire. Ma and Pa hid about six hundred dollars in gold, their entire savings, inside the upper berth mattress in the lead wagon.

Pa said we would drive out to the main road and then head south. He wanted to go down to Des Moines first to pick up a few supplies and a pair of new boots for each of us, and then we would pretty much drive west from there.

As we walked along, I noticed that Ma was crying.

"Ma, what's wrong?" I asked. "Are you okay?"

"Oh, I'm fine, Johnny. I'm just going to miss so many things about Polk City. I'm going to miss the garden. I'm especially going to miss my flowers—the dahlias and peonies. There will be flowers out in Nebraska too, I suppose."

Before we made it to the main road, Pa surprised us by pulling into the schoolyard, where Miss Baines was teaching class. Miss Baines let all the children come out and say their good-byes to us.

My friend Sam Hudson shook my hand. "Be seeing you, Captain Johnny." He handed me a shiny brass button tied to a string. "This button came from Daddy's uniform. He said that you could have it and wear it around your neck for good luck."

"Thanks Sam! Good luck fighting the Rebs, Captain. I'll handle any Confederate stragglers on the western frontier."

"Johnny, I don't think you need to worry about Rebels out there. I do think you might need to worry about Indians."

"Indians!"

"And they're for real, Johnny. Be careful."

"I'll be careful. Bye, Sam."

"Bye, Johnny."

I went up to Miss Baines, and she gave me a big hug. "You take care of your family, Johnny, and especially your little sister. I'm going to miss you all."

All the rest of us said our good-byes and then we were off to Des Moines. Our adventures had begun!

5
Des Moines

The excitement of being underway was considerably dampened by the presence of Eugene Dinwidden III. If anybody could make a dark cloud appear overhead in an otherwise bright blue sky, it was Eugene.

As we made our way out of Polk City, Kate and I were walking beside our wagon, and Ott and Elias were walking beside their wagon. Eugene was sitting in his wagon, arms folded and his face in a scowl.

"Why are you walking? Why aren't you riding?" shouted Eugene. "Isn't your wagon comfortable?"

"We're walking to make the load lighter for the horses," I said, trying to reason with him. "Pa said we should walk as much as we can. So, we're walking."

"Well, that's kind of stupid. I mean, why do we have wagons if we can't ride in 'em?"

"It's not stupid, Eugene. The horses are carrying a big load already as it is, with furniture and food and all our belongings. We can't wear 'em out before we get to Red Cloud."

"Suit yourself," said Eugene. "I'm not walking."

"We'll see how long their horses last," Pa said softly to

24

Ma. "And it isn't Eugene that I'm worried about."

I looked back at the Dinwidden's wagon. Mrs. Dinwidden and Miss O'Neill were both on the large side. Each of them probably weighed more than Mr. Dinwidden and Eugene put together. The two horses pulling that wagon had their work cut out for them.

Our wagon was being pulled by Millie and Billy, our old and faithful horses. We had a third horse, Blackie, tied to the rear of the wagon. Pa brought along Blackie as an extra in case one of the other horses took ill. Pa had also bought the two horses that were pulling the wagon that George was driving.

In addition to being our party's watchdog, Old Jack seemed to assume the title *Chaser of All Things Living.* He would walk with us and then disappear for quite awhile, scouring the countryside for rabbits and squirrels, and then he would appear again farther down the road.

We made it to Des Moines by early afternoon and pulled to a stop in front of a large general store.

"Why are we stopping here?" whined Eugene. "We could be making faster progress to Nebraska if we didn't stop."

"They're going to buy new shoes," said Mr. Dinwidden.

"I want a pair of new shoes, too," said Eugene.

"You already have a new pair of shoes, Eugene," said Mr. Dinwidden. "We bought those last week, remember?" he said, motioning to the pair Eugene was wearing.

"Oh, Gene, what's the harm in getting our boy another pair of shoes?" snapped Mrs. Dinwidden.

"Nonsense," said Mr. Dinwidden. "We'll wait in the wagon while they do their shoe shopping." The Dinwiddens and Miss O'Neill were still sitting in their wagon when the rest of us entered the store.

The store was immense, but Pa quickly and methodically helped us each select a new pair of boots, the first new shoes I ever had. They felt good on my feet—nice and warm, with no holes or cracks to allow in the cold air. Ma found a fabric that she liked, and she said she would use it to make dresses for herself and Kate. Pa paid for the shoes at two-and-a-half dollars per pair. The fabric was another dollar.

As we were walking out of the store, the store clerk called out, "Excuse me, but are you sure that you don't want to get wool socks to go with your new shoes?"

Pa turned, smiled, and shook his head. "No thanks," he said, and he turned back toward the door.

"Wait! We have a special sale starting next week, but I can give you the sale price today," said the clerk. Pa stopped and scratched his chin.

"Why don't you all go on back to the wagons," said Pa. "Catherine, let's have an early supper before we continue on. I'll talk with this gentleman and I'll either buy socks or I won't, and I'll be out in a few minutes."

When we returned to the wagons, we found Eugene holding a fistful of candy sticks. He had a ring of purple around his lips. "Look what I've got," he said in a taunting voice. "I have ten candy sticks. Daddy let me go in and buy them. They're grape. Grape is the best."

"Dorothy, Lucy," said Ma to Mrs. Dinwidden and Miss O'Neill, respectively, "we are going to have an early supper. You may want to eat something too, because I doubt we'll stop again until near nightfall. Children," she said, turning to us, "help me get supper ready. There's cooked chicken in the boiler, and we have bread and dried fruit."

Before we left Polk City, Ma had put the wash boiler on the stove and boiled up every chicken we owned. Then she filled up the boiler with salt brine to preserve the cooked chicken meat.

On the back of the lead wagon we had what most travelers called a grub box, but Ma refused to associate grubs with any of her food, so she called it a provision box. This helped remind us, too, that food was a provision from God.

The back side of the provision box flipped down, opening up the box and creating a table. There were drawers and shelves inside the box, and Ma had filled them with several loaves of home-baked bread, along with dried plums, apples, peaches, and some cherry and berry preserves.

Anyway, we had just started eating when Pa showed up carrying a box that was so large I could barely see his eyes over the top of it.

"Pa, what's in the box?" asked Kate.

"John, how many socks did you buy?" asked Ma.

Pa blushed. "Well, the socks were at a good price, and I figured that, with all the miles we'll be walking, we should have decent socks on our feet. So, I bought three pairs of socks for each person. And then I saw some other things I thought we could use."

"I'm afraid to ask," said Ma.

"Okay," said Pa, "each of us also gets a pair of dungarees and a new cotton shirt. They were a bargain price."

Ma shook her head. "That's the last time I leave you in a clothing store alone," she said, half-smiling. "Well, no harm done, I suppose. At least you didn't spend the money on candy."

"Oh … that reminds me," said Pa. He reached into his pocket and pulled out candy sticks. "They're root beer flavored," he said, handing one to each of us.

Ma sighed.

"Root beer flavored?" asked Eugene. "I want root beer flavored!" he demanded. "Daddy, go get me some root beer flavored candy sticks!"

Mr. Dinwidden, to his credit, just ignored Eugene.

After we finished eating, we continued on the journey. Pa wanted to get in a few more miles before we stopped for the evening. Eugene surprised all of us by deciding to walk with Kate and me. At least, he started off walking with us. He seemed to want to go faster than we were walking; he would dart ahead by ten or twenty feet and then look back over his shoulder with impatience and an air of superiority. He would wait until we caught up with him, and then he would do it again.

Finally he stopped, and with arms crossed he asked, "Come on, can't we go faster?"

"Eugene," said Pa, "we have a long ways to go. The horses have to be paced. We don't want to wear them down too much, or pretty soon they won't be going anywhere."

"But this is so slow!" whined Eugene.

"It seems like it, but I'll bet after doing this for the next few days you'll be wishing it wasn't so fast."

"How slow are we going?" asked Eugene, complaining more than asking.

"We may be going a little better than three miles every hour," said Pa.

"Oh, wonderful," said Eugene. "At this rate, I'll be an old man before we get to Nebraska."

Pa bit his lip but remained silent. After about an hour of walking, Eugene started griping that his feet were sore. "See, I told you I should have gotten new shoes!" he muttered as he climbed back into the wagon with Mr. and Mrs. Dinwidden.

We stopped late afternoon that first day, maybe four miles south of the confluence of the Raccoon and Des Moines rivers. We actually got a little farther along than Pa said he thought we would because the ground was frozen pretty hard, and the mud, which can be a problem for the wagon wheels, was of no consequence at all.

"George, build us a fire," said Pa. "It'll be good to warm our bones before bedding down for the night. You others can help me unload the wagons."

We had to remove our freight from the wagons each night so that we would have sleeping space. Each wagon's box was about three feet wide and ten feet long. The box proper was about fourteen inches tall, but Pa had added side-boards and cross-slats on the wagon box, making it ten inches taller and turning it into a sort of bunk bed— one mattress on top and one on the bottom.

Darkness comes quickly in February, and that evening was no exception. Ma lit the kerosene lanterns—each wagon had a lantern, made of either brass or glass, that hung from the ridge pole.

On that first night outside of Des Moines, the sleeping arrangements were straightforward. Ma and Pa slept in the lead wagon on the top berth. Kate and I slept on the bottom. Old Jack slept under the wagon on a bed we prepared for him. In the middle wagon, Mr. and Mrs. Dinwidden slept on the top berth and Eugene slept on the bottom berth with Miss O'Neill. In the third wagon,

George slept on the top berth and Elias and Ott slept on the bottom.

We slept in our clothes because we were too cold to think about removing them to put on night shirts.

The night was cold, no doubt about it, but we all wrapped ourselves in blankets, sticking noses out once in a while to get some fresh air, and we managed to stay warm enough.

"Johnny," Pa said to me the next morning, tapping me on the shoulder and waking me up, "I need you to gather firewood."

"We have firewood, Pa," I mumbled. "It's under the front seat of the wagon."

"I want to keep at least a two- or three-day supply under the front seat," he said.

"Yes sir," I said, crawling out of the wagon.

"I'll help you find wood, Johnny," said Kate, descending to the ground right after me.

Kate and I returned minutes later, each bearing an armload of sticks in assorted sizes.

"Very good," said Pa. "Put as much of the wood as you can in the front wagon, and put the rest in George's. How would you two like to be in charge of our wood supply for this trip? You could be our wood elves."

"Sure, Pa!" we both exclaimed.

Kate turned to me and whispered, "Johnny, this wood elf job will be a cinch. It's so easy to find wood by the side of the road."

I didn't know if Pa heard Kate, but he said, "Oh, just in case you think gathering wood in Iowa is easy, I should tell you that it may be much more difficult once we get to

Nebraska. I've heard Nebraska has a lot fewer trees. Being a wood elf may turn out to be a most challenging job."

Cold and hungry, I sidled up to a fire Ott had built, and I basked in the heat while also enjoying the aromas emanating from the skillet of bacon and eggs that Ma was cooking.

Miss O'Neill was also awake and was preparing breakfast for the Dinwiddens. The Dinwiddens seemed to be just waking up. They were lucky to have her.

Pa had long been in the habit of giving each of us a teaspoon of his special tonic every morning. Even though Pa would dilute the tonic considerably with water and would sometimes add sugar, it still would give our heads a good shake. He said the alcohol opened our pores and forced out any illness. I wasn't so sure about that, but it may have worked. At least, any kid named Stevens was rarely out of school for any reason.

So, that morning, Pa gave us each a spoonful, and then we all set to work. We packed the wagons while Pa and George repaired a cracked spoke in one of the wheels.

I could tell by the look on Eugene's face that he was going to have a grumpy day, and that did not portend well for the rest of us. But, grumpy passengers or not, we loaded up the wagons and headed toward the town of Indianola. The ground remained frozen and hard, and we seemed to be moving at a pretty good clip as we began the second day on the road.

Eugene was about as bad as I expected. That pest of a boy complained about lack of sleep; he complained about being cold; he complained that his food was not cooked just right; and he complained that no one seemed to be willing to take care of him. He whined that he had to leave Polk City. He whined that we weren't already in Nebraska. He whined that we couldn't just take the train. And he whined that he had to follow someone else's schedule.

Finally, Kate turned to him and said, "Eugene, be quiet! If you can't say anything without complaining, then you shouldn't say anything at all. But the way I look at it is like this. Today is a new day with new adventures, and I'm excited to find out what they are. We're all going to Nebraska and we may as well be excited about it. Whining and complaining aren't going to change anything. So just make the best of it, Eugene."

Pa, who had been keeping quiet while Eugene was on his tirade, turned around and said, "Kate, there's a whole lot of wisdom in what you're saying. Yes, it's exciting to discover what God has in store for us."

Eugene was silent at that point. I think he was mad at Kate, and he wasn't going to talk to her. He was also mad at me. But I think that he really didn't know what to think. He hadn't figured out yet that a person needs to try to make the best out of any situation.

6

Indianola

Johnny, whatcha got hangin' from your neck?" asked Eugene Dinwidden III, as we tromped along toward Indianola, Iowa.

"Oh, it's just a gift from Sam."

"How come Sam didn't give me a gift?"

"You weren't Sam's friend."

"He wouldn't be my friend," whined Eugene.

"No Eugene, you're remembering that backwards. Sam and I—and pretty much everyone else—all tried to be your friends. Actually, I'm still trying."

"Well, can I see it?" asked Eugene, extending a hand toward the button.

"No, not right now. Hands off," I said.

"Johnny," I heard a low voice say behind me, "he can see the button."

"Yes, Pa," I said. I pulled off the string with the button from around my neck and handed it to Eugene.

"Wow, this is nice," Eugene said. "I like it. Do you have any more of these? Do you know where I can get one?"

"Um … no … I don't know. I'll take it back now," I said, grabbing the button and putting it back around my neck, not waiting for a reply.

"I wasn't done looking at it," said Eugene. "Give it back, Johnny Stevens!"

I needed a distraction, some way to get Eugene's mind off of the button.

"Sixty-one thousand five hundred ten," I said out loud, followed seconds later with, "Sixty-one thousand five hundred twenty."

"Johnny, what in the sand hills are you doing?"

"I'm counting footsteps, Eugene. Step 61,530."

"Counting footsteps?"

"Yes, indeed. I decided when we left Polk City that it would be really interesting—61,540—to count every step I made from Iowa to Nebraska."

"Why didn't you tell me you were doing that? I want to do it too! But now it's too late. Not fair," he pouted.

"Step 61,550. I didn't think you'd find it fun. It's a whole lot more fun, though, than I thought it would be. Step 61,560."

"If I do it, do I have to start at zero?"

"Tell you what, Eugene. Start with my count—61,570—and then just add your own steps to it. I find it easiest to add every ten steps—61,580—but suit yourself. Whatever works for you."

For the next four hours, the only words coming from Eugene's lips were numbers, and even those were few. Eugene counted silently almost the entire way.

When we reached the north side of Indianola, we stopped for the night in what was obviously a camping area—large and flat, marked by a dozen or so fire pits where past travelers had built campfires, and with a nearby stream.

Pa stepped out of the wagon, squeezed me on the

shoulder, and in a low voice said, "Brilliant, Johnny. Simply brilliant."

"So, Eugene," began Kate, "how many steps have you taken?"

Eugene said, "Well … uh … um … Johnny, how many steps did you get?"

"Eugene, I'm at 144,100," I said.

"Right. I'm at 144,050. That's because I take smaller steps than you do," said Eugene.

"But that would mean you need to take more steps, not fewer steps, since we went the same distance."

"Oh, I meant I'm at 144,150 steps. Yes, that's right. My count is 144,150 steps."

Another wagon was there too, maybe a hundred yards away, with a husband and wife in their early forties. As we were setting up camp, the man from the other wagon approached us.

"Afternoon," he said.

"Afternoon," replied Pa.

"James Stilton, Waukon," said the man.

"John Stevens, Polk City," said Pa.

Pa was always cautious around strangers, which explains the riveting conversation. It reminded me of two big dogs meeting for the first time, each trying to determine if the other was friend or foe.

"Where ya headed?" asked the man.

"Western Nebraska. You?"

"South, to St. Louis," said the man. "We camped here last night too. My wife and I, we went into town earlier today and looked around Indianola."

"Nice town, isn't it?" said Pa, more telling than asking.

"Been here before?"

"Once or twice, but not recently."

"Yeah, it's friendly. Anyway, they've got a town band that supposedly is pretty good, and they're giving a concert tomorrow, weather permitting, in the town square."

"What time?" asked Pa.

"Around noon," said the man.

"Thanks for letting me know. I'll think about it."

"Pleasure meeting you, Mr. Stevens," said the man.

"Pleasure's mine, Mr. Stilton," said Pa.

Ma, who had been getting food out of the provision box, turned and said to Pa, "Might be nice to give our young travelers a rest for the morning. Besides, it's not often that we get to hear a band play."

"That sounds fine to me," said Pa.

"Ma, do you want us to set up the little stove for supper?" asked Ott. The little stove was a small sheet metal stove, light-weight and easy to move. It was carried in the third wagon and we used it when we didn't have the inclination, time, or enough dry fuel to light a campfire. The stove didn't require as much wood as a campfire, but it also didn't provide the amount of body-warming heat that we enjoyed with a campfire. Our regular stove, too heavy and cumbersome to take out of the wagon during our trip west, was packed in the lead wagon.

"No, Ott, that won't be necessary. We'll cook supper with a campfire," said Ma.

George built the fire; Ma and Miss O'Neill made dinner; we all helped clean up; and we were in bed by the time darkness set in.

It seemed like no time had passed before I felt Pa's hand on my shoulder, waking me up. Kate and I gathered firewood and then helped Ma prepare our breakfast of cornmeal mush.

When breakfast was nearly ready, Ma said, "Before we eat, we're going to wash up a bit. This is the warmest morning we have seen in a while, and I think we should take advantage of the opportunity that God has given us to wash the dirt off our faces, necks and behind our ears. Boys and Kate, hop to it."

Why did Ma always tell us to wash behind our ears? It wasn't like people walked around looking behind other people's ears.

Anyway, I got in line behind George, Elias, Ott, and Kate. When it was my turn, I partially unbuttoned my shirt and then I took off my string with the button and set it on a tree stump. I started washing my face. The morning air was chilly but not as cold as it had been, and it felt good to clean up, even though I would remain in the same clothing I had been wearing.

"Breakfast is ready," Ma called out just as I was finishing. I threw the towel over a rope that we had strung between two wagons, buttoned up my shirt and put on my coat, and sat down with a warm bowl of cornmeal mush in hand.

After breakfast, we loaded up the wagons and headed into Indianola. Kate, Eugene, and I walked alongside the lead wagon.

"I think hearing the band will be fun, Johnny," said Eugene, smiling. I stared at Eugene a moment—his statement was completely out of character for him—and then nodded in agreement.

"Don't you love bands, Johnny? I love bands. I have always loved bands. I can't wait to hear the band, Johnny."

I knew that something was up with Eugene, but I didn't know what. He just seemed uncommonly happy.

The road going into town led straight to the Town Square, where people were already gathering under a sign that read: Indianola Musical Club and Brass Band.

"When will the concert start, Mother?" asked Eugene.

"Well, how would I know?" snapped Mrs. Dinwidden, annoyed.

"It will start right after the church bell rings at noon," said a gentleman sitting in front of us, turning around and smiling. "I take it you all are visiting?"

"Just passing through," said Pa.

The church bells began ringing—twelve rings—and then the band started playing. They played marches and hymns, some slow and some fast, some loud and some soft. Miss O'Neill especially seemed to enjoy it. She was tapping her foot and clapping to the rhythm.

At one point, she leaned over and said to me, "This just makes me want to get up and dance! I wonder what the occasion is?"

The man in front of us turned around again and said, "Pardon me, ma'am, I was not intending to eavesdrop, but I heard your question. This isn't for any special occasion. These fellas in the band just like getting together every month or so, and they play outdoors, when weather permits, for all of us to enjoy. Of course, it's rare that we get to hear them outdoors in the winter months."

The concert ended in grand style with a fiery march that made goose bumps rise on the back of my neck.

"Pa, what's that big instrument?" I asked, pointing to something much larger than the other instruments.

"That is a ... well, I'm not really sure," said Pa.

"That is a tuba," said the man in front of us. "It's the largest of the brass instruments, and it makes the lowest sounds. Would you like to go up and see it?"

"Could I?" I asked.

"I'm a friend of the tuba player. Come on."

I looked at Pa, who nodded. I walked with the man over to the platform. The tuba player was putting his instrument back into a case.

"Wales," said the man, "Wales, this young boy is interested in the tuba."

"Well, hello there," said the large man with a booming voice. "My name is Puffer, Wales Puffer. I run the local feed store two blocks over, but if I could make a livin' playin' tuba, yes sir, that's what I'd be doing."

"Nice to meet you, Mr. Puffer," I said.

"Put her there," he said, and we shook hands.

"Does it take a lot of air to play that?" I asked.

"Well, the only way for you to find out is to try it. Go ahead, sit down in the chair."

I sat down. He picked up the tuba and put it in my lap. It was heavy.

"Now, young man, put your lips against the mouthpiece and blow as hard as you can."

I took a deep breath, pressed my lips against the mouthpiece, and blew as hard as I could. Nothing came out except the swish of a small wind. I took another deep breath and tried again. Nothing. I tried yet a third time, and again, no noise.

"This is hard!" I exclaimed. "How do you get enough air to make a sound?"

"Well, it's practice. It's not just about how much air, it's also about focusing the air stream so that the air is more concentrated in the right place in the mouthpiece."

"Kind of like whistling?"

"Uh, no, not really," he said. "Press your lips together so that they're sealed tight. Then try to push air out of your mouth—use your lungs and stomach to push the air—and loosen your lips just enough to let a little air through."

I did what he said, and a low-pitched blat came out of the tuba! It wasn't pretty, but it was a real sound.

"Johnny, that sounded pitiful. In fact, it was horrible," said Eugene, who had walked up behind me.

I pretended I hadn't heard Eugene's comment. "Mr. Puffer, thank you for letting me try," I said. Mr. Puffer lifted the tuba from my lap.

"I'll bet I could do it," Eugene boasted, stepping between Mr. Puffer and me. "You looked so silly, Johnny, blowing into it with no sound coming out."

I didn't really know how to respond to Eugene.

He turned and faced me. "Father says I've got music in my blood. I don't think you've got any music in your blood, Johnny. Otherwise, you'd be able to play that thing."

Eugene had turned so that Mr. Puffer was behind him. While Eugene was going on and on about my lack of musical ability, Mr. Puffer quietly picked up his tuba, placed the big bell (where the sound comes out) right behind Eugene's head, and took a deep breath.

BLAST! The tuba roared. Eugene was so startled that he fell off the edge of the platform. He landed on soft grass.

"Oh, most sorry, young master, I didn't see you there," said Mr. Puffer, with a twinkle in his eye.

"I hate brass bands!" Eugene stomped off in a fit.

"Well, if that young man didn't have music in his blood before, he certainly does now," said Mr. Puffer, laughing.

After we returned to the wagons, we found a dry area and sat down on the ground to eat a meal of bread and cheese before heading toward our next destination, Osceola, Iowa.

We traveled toward Osceola for nearly four hours and then stopped to set up camp for the night. Pa thought we were not quite halfway between Indianola and Osceola.

"How many steps, Johnny?" asked Eugene.

"Oh, I think I'm at 210,870. You?"

"Why … um … that would be 210,970 for me."

It was sometime after we stopped that day that I realized my button was missing! The string wasn't around my neck. I thought hard to when I had last seen it. I had taken it off when we were washing, right before eating breakfast that morning in Indianola.

I recalled hearing Ma say that breakfast was ready, and I had hung up the towel and then buttoned my shirt quickly. I must have left the button on the stump.

I told Ma and Pa, and we all ended up looking around the campsite for it, just in case. We didn't find it though. I felt sad. I was also mad at myself for losing the button; it felt as though I had betrayed Sam.

Miss O'Neill walked over and gave me a hug. "I'll be looking for it, Johnny."

"It's no use, Miss O'Neill. I'm pretty sure I left the button on a tree stump in Indianola."

"I'll keep my eyes open just the same," she said. "I saw a white horse in a field we passed by this afternoon."

"White horse? What does that mean?"

"My granddaddy always said that if you make a wish on a white horse, the wish might come true. I hadn't made a wish yet, but now I have."

"Miss O'Neill, I don't—"

"Shh, Johnny. Don't say it. It's fun to hope, anyway."

I smiled. "Okay, Miss O'Neill. We can hope."

7
Osceola

Boom! The sound of a shotgun blast not too far in the distance woke me up.

"What's going on?" I asked, lifting my head up and hitting it with a thud on the wood slat supporting the bed above me.

"Ouch, that must have hurt," said Kate, stirring next to me.

"Serves me right for sitting up without thinking first," I said, rubbing my head. "Did you hear that gunshot?"

Kate yawned. "Yes, I did. Elias talked about getting up early this morning to hunt pheasant and quail. Sounded like his gun. Anyway, it's time to get up, I suppose."

Kate and I crawled out of bed just as Elias was returning to the camp. He laid down his rifle in the back of his wagon and proudly held up the pheasant he had shot.

"Got us some dinner, Pa!" he exclaimed.

"Nice shootin', son," said Pa. He and Ma had been up for a while. Pa was building a campfire, and Ma was standing next to a tree that had a large piece of cloth hanging from one of the lower branches.

"What is that, Ma? Looks like a bed sheet."

"No, it's Mrs. Dinwidden's dress," said Ma in a soft

43

voice, "the one that she wore to the concert we went to yesterday. It was soiled, so she washed it last night before we went to bed and I was just checking to see how close it is to being dry."

Kate whispered, "But she couldn't possibly have gotten dirty at the concert. We were sitting on benches."

Ma motioned to us to come closer.

"Remember the picnic we had afterward, before we left Indianola? We were sitting on the ground. City folks don't always think to check where they sit. People forget that Iowa has cows," said Ma with a slight twinkle in her eye.

"You mean ... Mrs. Dinwidden sat on a cow pattie?" I could feel myself start to giggle, and I had to put my hands to my face to keep from bursting out in laughter. "Was it," I began, struggling to keep a straight face, "was it an old, dried pattie, or was it ... fresh?"

Ma's face turned red as she tried to refrain from laughing. "It was ... fresh," said Ma.

"Johnny, Kate, fetch me some kindling from the wagon," said Pa. Kate and I dutifully obliged and were at the front of our wagon, still snickering about Mrs. Dinwidden's dress, when we heard Pa shout, "Eugene!"

I turned my head only to see Eugene, walking around from behind the third wagon, brandishing a shotgun and carelessly pointing it in Ma's general direction.

"Eugene," said Pa sternly, "that is Elias's gun. Set it down."

"Look at me, folks," Eugene said with a smile. "I'm a regular cowboy!"

"Eugene, drop the—"

BOOM!

The gun discharged. The kickback from the shotgun blast knocked Eugene off of his feet. I looked toward Ma—she was lying on the ground!

"Catherine!" shouted Pa, leaping up and running toward Ma.

Within seconds, the rest of us were huddled around Pa and Ma. Pa cradled his hands behind Ma's head, lifting it slightly. Ma was totally limp.

"Catherine … Catherine can you hear me?" asked Pa. There was no response.

"Johnny," said Pa, turning to me, "get me some clean rags. And hurry!"

"Yes sir," I said, quickly running to the lead wagon because I knew that was where Ma kept clean rags. When I returned, Pa was kneeling over Ma, saying a prayer.

"… and Lord, we know that we only need to be still and that you will do the fighting for us. Lord, we trust in you for this healing, this miracle. Heal our lack of trust. Amen."

I saw the stain of blood on Pa's hands.

"Pa," I began, "is … is …"

"Ma is still breathing, praise be to God. There's only a little blood, and it didn't come from the shotgun. I think she hit the back of her head on a rock when she fell."

"Pa, look, Ma's arm is moving!" said Kate.

"Catherine, can you hear me?" asked Pa.

Ma opened her eyes. "John … what … what happened?"

It was then that Pa remembered Eugene. I could hear the anger in his voice rising as he said, "Well, I think we have an impudent, spoiled, little brat on this trip who needs a good whipping."

"That's right … I remember now," said Ma. "When

Eugene came around the corner carrying the shotgun and I saw it pointed right at me, I backed away and tripped. That's all I remember."

Pa and Miss O'Neill worked together to get Ma bandaged up. The bleeding was minor, but Ma said her head ached.

Pa walked over to the wagon, picked up a hickory switch that he would occasionally use on the horses to keep them motivated, and he walked toward Eugene with a somber look on his face.

"Eugene," said Pa softly, "this could have turned out much worse … much, much worse."

"I'm … the gun shouldn't have been loaded, that's all I can say," said Eugene.

Pa looked at Mr. Dinwidden and said, "Gene, if you won't do it, I will."

"I will do it," said Mr. Dinwidden, taking the switch from Pa. Mr. Dinwidden took a firm hold on Eugene's shoulder and said, "Come with me." As the two of them walked off into the woods, I could hear Mr. Dinwidden reprimanding Eugene: "I've told you a hundred times to never pick up a gun. That's why we don't have any guns on our wagon!"

I don't know how hard Mr. Dinwidden laid into Eugene with that switch, but judging from the whelps and cries I heard coming from the woods, I suspected that Eugene wouldn't feel any urge to sit down for a good week or so.

"Catherine, let's stay here another day so that you can get some rest," said Pa.

"No, John, I feel fine. I really do. My head is throbbing only a little," said Ma.

"Now Catherine—"

"John, I really believe I will do better if we can keep moving, keep making forward progress toward Nebraska."

"You're a stubborn old mule," said Pa.

"Takes one to know one," said Ma, laughing.

"All right, then," said Pa, "let's eat some breakfast and we'll load up and be on our way."

"Oh, Catherine," said Mrs. Dinwidden, "have you seen my dress? It is nowhere to be found."

Ma glanced at where Mrs. Dinwidden had hung the dress to dry, but it wasn't there. Ma sent Kate to look for it, and Kate found the dress on the ground behind a bush, a few feet away. She brought the dress to Mrs. Dinwidden.

Mrs. Dinwidden held the dress up for examination. The fabric had been shredded by the shotgun blast, and there was a big hole where none had existed before.

"Gene!" shouted Mrs. Dinwidden. "Gene! Where is that hickory switch?"

We made good progress that day and drove the final sixteen miles to Osceola, reaching the town by mid-afternoon.

"Johnny, what does Osceola mean?" asked Kate, as we made our way through the town.

"It's an Indian word, Kate. I'm not sure what it means, but there was a Seminole Indian named Osceola, and I think the town was named after him."

"Indians! Well, they'd better not try to mess with us. Johnny, do Seminole Indians live around here?"

"I don't think so, Kate. I think they're from Florida. Maybe Osceola came up to Iowa for summer vacations."

Kate smiled.

We were passing through town when Pa decided to stop at a general store. He said he wanted to talk with someone about crossing the Missouri.

While we were waiting beside the wagons, two

children—a boy and a girl about the ages of Kate and me—stepped out of the general store and seemed to be headed across the street.

"Johnny, Kate, I think they are Indians," whispered Eugene.

"How do you know that, Eugene?"

"I don't know how I know, but I'm sure of it. Why don't you ask them, Kate?"

Before I could stop Kate, she blurted out, "Excuse me, but are you Indians?"

The boy and girl glanced at each other and then walked toward us.

Eugene said, "Say something to them."

Kate spoke.

"Me Kate. Me called Kate," she said, loudly and slowly.

The boy and girl stared at Kate. The boy spoke slowly. "Kate. You called Kate."

Kate pointed to the girl and asked, "She called what?"

The boy looked confused at first, but then smiled. He pointed to the girl standing next to him and said loudly, "She called What."

"No, I mean, I don't know name," said Kate.

"You called Kate."

"I know my name is Kate," replied Kate. "What her name?"

"Her name What," the boy answered.

"Oh dear, I've muddled everything up," sighed Kate. "Let me try this again. Who are you?"

The boy pause for a few seconds and then responded, "I called Who?"

"Uh, no," said Kate. "You called what?"

"She called What!" declared the boy.

"I have an idea," said Kate. "Me called what?" She shrugged her shoulders, hoping that was a common sign for asking a question. Then she answered the question by saying, "Me called Kate."

And again, slowly and loudly, Kate repeated, "Me called what? Me called Kate."

The boy hesitated a moment, looked at the little girl, and then looked back at Kate with the bright eyes of one who has come to an understanding. Then, in perfect English, he answered, "Ah, I understand now! My name is William Danforth, and this is my little sister, Amelia Danforth. We have lived here in Osceola all our lives—I am ten and she is seven. Whereabouts are you from?"

Kate's eyes were almost as big as saucers. "We're … we're from Polk City," she said.

"Polk City! Polk City!" said William Danforth, eyes opened wide. "Amelia, did you hear that? They are from Polk City!" He paused and, in a serious tone, asked, "Now, just exactly where is Polk City? Folks from Polk City sure do talk funny."

The boy and the girl both laughed, and they ran off. When Kate realized they had made fun of her, she started pouting a bit.

"Kate," said Ma, who saw and heard the whole thing, "you can't fault the children for wanting to have some fun. They wouldn't have teased you like that if they didn't like you."

"Okay Ma, it's okay. They just caught me off guard. I really thought at first that they were Indians."

As we began making our way out of Osceola, Kate asked me, "Did you hear them? Did you hear them speak, Johnny?"

"Well, yes Kate, I did." I was puzzled.

"We're so far from Polk City, but they sounded just like we do!" she exclaimed in excitement.

"Well, shouldn't they? I mean, after all, we're still in the same state—Iowa. I believe that people don't start talking funny until you're at least a whole state away. I'll bet you almost anything, Kate, that we'll have a tough time understanding the fine citizens of south central Nebraska. Who knows? They may even have their own totally separate alphabet."

We camped that night just west of Osceola. The air was feeling cold again, and the wind was picking up from the west.

As we were cleaning up after supper, Miss O'Neill said, "It smells like snow's coming tonight."

She was right.

8
Creston

Sometimes a snow storm stampedes across the plains in a furious rage, a herd of buffalo bent on destruction. But sometimes the snow subtly, quietly settles in like an old, gentle cat, content to do nothing more than sleep on your lap. That was the kind of snow that sneaked into our camp in the middle of the night.

When we woke up the next morning, we found that a blanket of white had covered everything we could see that wasn't protected from the elements. Tree branches were laced with four or five inches of snow, as were the tops of the wagon covers. Fortunately the wind wasn't blowing hard and the temperature wasn't all that cold. In fact, the skies had already turned blue and it looked like it would be a nice day.

With little fanfare, we ate, loaded up, and set out for the town of Creston, straight west of Osceola. Pa said it was a little more than thirty miles away and that it would take us at least two days to get there.

Ott began whistling a tune, and moments later he broke out into a song:

> *Excuse me, Sir, I have something to ask ya,*
> *You ever heard of a state called Nebraska?*

That's where the corn grows mighty tall
And the milo's the sweetest of all.
Have you ever been to Nebraska?
Just thought I'd ask ya,
Just thought I'd ask ya.

Excuse me, Sir, I have something to ask ya,
You ever heard of a state called Nebraska?
That's where the boys are lean and strong
And the folks won't do you no wrong.
Have you ever been to Nebraska?
Just thought I'd ask ya,
Just thought I'd ask ya.

"Where'd you learn that song?" asked Kate.

"Learn it? I didn't," said Ott.

"What do you mean that you didn't learn it?"

"I just made it up."

"You just made it up right now?"

"Yes ma'am, just right now."

"Could you sing more?"

"I reckon I could," said Ott. He continued:

Excuse me, Sir, I have something to ask ya,
You ever heard of a state called Nebraska?
They say the girls are all first rate,
Especially one that goes by Kate.
Have you ever been to Nebraska?
Just thought I'd ask ya,
Just thought I'd ask ya.

Kate smiled and began humming the tune herself. "I think I like that song, Ott."

The day's journey went quickly. That afternoon, after we stopped for the day and were getting things set up for supper, Kate and I went out to perform our duties as wood elves. All the wood we found was wet, but we still gathered it because we figured the wood would dry out over the next couple of days. We had asked Eugene if he wanted to come help, but he was snooty about it and said he didn't feel like helping. Kate and I brought back the wood we had found and were putting it under the front seat of the wagon when—PLUNK—a snowball hit me in the back! I picked up the still intact ball, turned, and—it was Pa! I launched the snowball with all my might, and it hit Pa in the shoulder.

"Ouch!" he yelled, and then he smiled. "I guess I deserved that one."

Within moments, the rest of the family and Miss O'Neill all joined in the snowball fight. We took sides and it turned into an all-out war. Ott, Kate, and I teamed up and we held our own against everybody else. Well, almost everybody else. I noticed that the Dinwidden family just stood and watched. They didn't seem to know what to do, how to play in the snow. I felt sorry for them.

The next day—our sixth day since leaving Polk City— it snowed from sunup to sundown, and it was cold. The worst part wasn't the snow, it was the wind. We marched into a grueling headwind the entire way. Even Old Jack wanted to ride in the wagon.

Exhausted, we made it to the edge of Creston by late afternoon and found a vacant camp site.

Just when we were sitting down for supper, Ott returned from tending to the horses.

"Pa," said Ott, "I think Millie's got a bad leg. She's favoring it."

"Let me take a look," said George. He jumped to his feet and walked over to Millie.

Moments later, George walked back to the campfire. "Ott is right. She's favoring her leg. I 'spect she just needs a rest."

"Let's do this, then," said Pa. "We'll take a rest day tomorrow. I'd like to walk into town in the morning. I'll need George, Elias, and Ott to stay here and keep an eye on things, but I thought that the younger folks—Johnny, Kate, and Eugene—might want to walk with me down to the train station and look around. The Creston train station is one of the biggest stations this side of the Mississippi."

"The train station!" exclaimed Kate. "That sounds fun."

Creston bustled in a flurry of activity as we entered the town the next morning. I saw storefronts with signs hanging for all kinds of establishments—banks, lawyers, apothecaries, and the like—and the streets were filled with people milling about.

Pa led us to the train station. When I asked him how he had known where to go, he smiled and said, "Just followed the tracks."

I had never seen so many train tracks in all my life, and it seemed like they headed off in every direction. Across the railroad yard from the depot stood a large, round building with tracks leading to it. "What's that building, Pa?"

A booming voice surprised us from behind.

"Whoa, there!" said a big, bearded man. "Youngsters?

Do I see inquisitive children? Yes I do, indeed! Might these be future conductors or engineers who would like to see a train?" He gave a hearty, boisterous laugh.

We smiled at him, not quite sure what to say.

"Cat got your tongue?" he teased. "Would you all like to have a tour of the inside of a train?"

Our eyes opened in anticipation. "Oh Pa, can we, please?"

"I think that would be fine. I'd like to see it too."

"George King is my name," said the man, extending his hand toward Pa, "retired railroad engineer who just can't stay away from the old place." Pa shook his hand.

"Yes sir, the kind folks here at the station have allowed this old man to stick around, giving tours and chuckles to visitors." His bright red cheeks somehow reminded me of St. Nicholas.

"Now," he continued, "I heard this young master here asking about the roundhouse. The roundhouse is basically a building with a big, flat wheel in the floor that you can put a train engine on, turn the wheel, and point the train off in another direction. Our roundhouse here in Creston is the largest this side of Chicago."

Mr. King then proceeded to tell us what must have been pretty near everything there was to know about trains. He also told stories of armed train robberies, Indian attacks, and some of the famous people he had met on his travels.

"Mr. King, why did the railroad decide that it should run through Creston?" I asked.

"That's a good question, young man," said Mr. King.

Eugene snorted. I noticed that Mr. King gave Eugene a quick glance, but he kept right on talking.

Mr. King said, "About a dozen or so years ago, a group

of folks was building the Burlington-Missouri Railroad. Of course, folks working on the railroad needed a place to eat and sleep. They made railroad camps, and eventually some of those railroad camps became towns. The camp here became Creston."

He led us to a train engine, and he said, "You can climb up and step inside the door, but for safety reasons I must ask you not to touch anything."

Kate, Eugene, and I climbed up and stepped inside the door. We looked around for a minute or so, until we were content that we had seen enough.

As we prepared to climb down from the engine, Kate pointed and said, "Look Johnny, that's the train whistle!" She motioned to a rope hanging down from some kind of lever. "How hard do you suppose that is to pull?" she asked.

"I don't know, Kate. I think you have to be pretty strong."

"I'll bet I could do it," said Eugene.

"I'll bet you couldn't," said Kate.

Without further argument, Eugene jumped up and grabbed the rope, pulling down with all his might.

I put my hands over my ears, but nothing happened. I guessed the train had to be running in order for the whistle to work.

"I was sure I could do it," said a dejected Eugene. I didn't tell him that it might have worked if the train engine had been running.

A little bit later on the tour, Mr. King took us right next to a train engine that was already running. That engine was humming and it sounded smooth and powerful.

Out of the corner of my eye, I could see Mr. King signal something to the engineer on the train.

CHOO CHOOOOOOOOOOOO!

The whistle blasted, startling all of us, including me, who even suspected it was coming. Eugene was so surprised that he almost fell to the ground.

"Ho ho, did that surprise you?" chortled Mr. King.

"That wasn't funny," said Eugene with a scowling face.

"Just having a bit of fun," said Mr. King.

"Well, have fun with somebody else," said Eugene, stomping away in anger. That boy needed a good scolding.

As we were falling asleep that night, Kate turned toward me and whispered, "Johnny?"

"Yeah?"

"Why is Eugene so stubborn and disobedient?"

"I don't know, Kate."

"Seems like it'll get him in trouble someday."

"Sure does, Kate."

That day came sooner than any of us expected.

9
Thin Ice

I wasn't sure how long I could keep the step-counting ruse going. Eugene was beginning to catch on, and while it kept him occupied, I think it stopped being the successful distraction it had been. I tried it one more time as we left Creston and set our sights on the town of Corning, Iowa.

"Eugene, I'm at 602,500 steps. How about you?"

"Oh bother, Johnny, I'm tired of counting steps. It takes all my concentration just to remember the numbers, and I can't think of anything else. I'm not counting any more."

Later, we had stopped for the evening and were setting up for supper when Mr. and Mrs. Dinwidden noticed that Eugene was missing. They asked me if I had seen him, and I said no but that I would help go look for him. They resumed whatever they were doing before, apparently taking my response to mean that they expected me do all the work to find him.

I saw tracks in the snow that seemed to be heading toward a field, and they looked to be about the size of Eugene's footsteps. I followed them. They led me across the field and toward a thicket of trees. The tracks wound their way down into a small ravine and then alongside a frozen brook. I followed the tracks around a bend, where the trees cleared to reveal a pond. There I found Eugene, sliding along on top of the ice!

"Eugene," I called out. "I don't think that pond is safe." Even with the snow, the days had been warm enough that I knew the ice might not be all that solid.

"Oh, go away," shouted Eugene. "I'm having fun and I want to be by myself. The pond is fine. It's frozen all the way through."

"Eugene, it's not safe. I'm telling you, I know about these things."

The truth of the matter was that I wasn't sure if it was safe or not, but Pa always told me, "When you're not sure, assume it's not safe."

"Oh hogwash, it's safe. Johnny, you're a sissy."

At that moment, I heard a sharp, cracking sound, and then another, and in horror I watched Eugene plummet with a big splash through the surface of the pond. He was totally submerged. It occurred to me that I had no idea whether Eugene could swim, but I was guessing that he couldn't.

I crawled out on the ice to where Eugene had broken through, and I reached down into the cold water. Eugene was nowhere to be found. I was hoping he would bounce back up so that all I would have to do was pull him out. But he wasn't coming up. I did the only thing I could think of doing. Pulling off my boots and my coat—I knew they would weigh me down—I lowered myself into the water.

The pain of the ice water seared through my body; it felt as if my lungs were collapsing and I couldn't breathe. I reached out with my arms and legs, but I couldn't find Eugene. I knew I had to go underwater and I tried to take a deep breath first, but my lungs couldn't find any breath. I decided to go under anyway.

Under the surface, I opened my eyes. The cold water stung, but I saw something flash to my left, something that caught a glint of the little bit of sunlight that remained. In desperation, I reached for it. It was Eugene!

He was thrashing and struggling, and he pulled himself up on my body in an attempt to reach the surface. I let him climb, and then with all my might I kicked my legs to propel both of us back to the surface.

We gasped as soon as our faces were above the surface, and Eugene was spitting out water. We had to get out of the pond. I pushed him to the edge of the ice where it had broken. It was hard getting him up onto the ice, partly because the ice was so slippery but also because it was breaking more as we put weight on it. Slowly, though, I was able to push Eugene up out of the water. I'm not sure how—my hands and feet couldn't feel anything. Then I managed to climb out.

Eugene was coughing and shivering. I slid my feet into my boots and then I wrapped my coat around Eugene. I told him to get on my back, and he did, but it was hard for him to hold on to me. I wanted to get out of the woods and into the open field where someone might see us.

We started walking and suddenly Pa's words echoed in my mind—*just follow the tracks*. I found our snow tracks. The cold numbness made it hard for me to lift my legs, and I tripped on some branches, falling forward with Eugene on top of me. I stood back up, he climbed on my back, and we kept going. I hadn't walked more than twenty feet before I fell again. Panic raced through my mind. What if we didn't make it back and were never found?

I thought back to a scene a year or two earlier, when Pa and I were sitting by the fireplace on a cold Iowa night. I remembered Pa telling me, "Son, if you ever find yourself lost out in the cold Iowa snow, never stop walking, never stop going one direction, trying to be found. You might feel tired and want to sleep. But don't stop, don't ever stop."

Don't ever stop. Those words rang through my head. Pulling Eugene back up, I dragged him with me toward the edge of the woods. I could see the large, open field up ahead through the trees, and that became my target; if only we could make it to that field. I struggled carrying Eugene through the woods; low hanging branches were striking my face and clawing at my clothes, as if they were trying to hold me back. I tripped and fell again, and I vaguely heard Eugene whimpering.

I got back up somehow, but I started feeling sleepy, and I was wondering why I had gotten up off the ground. It seemed like rest was what I needed. *Don't ever stop.* I heard those words again. *But Pa*, I wanted to shout, *I feel so tired.* I just wanted to sleep a little while. The coldness was fading—in fact, I was beginning to feel comfortable.

Don't ever stop. I wasn't sure if I was moving or not; was I still walking, or was I lying down and falling asleep? Where was Eugene? Was I carrying him? *Don't ever ...*

The next thing I remember is that I was sitting by the fire, wrapped in blankets, with Ma, Elias, and Ott rubbing my arms and my legs. I was still cold, numb, and shivering, but I was in dry clothing. I remember Elias looking at me as he said, "You're going to be all right, Johnny." Then he kissed me on the forehead.

"Where's Eugene?" I asked.

"Right there," said Ma, pointing to the other side of the fire, where Eugene was wrapped up in his mother's arms.

Eugene's lips were blue, and I suspected that mine were as well. Pa got out his big bottle of tonic, and for once I didn't object to the nasty, horrid concoction. I knew it would help me feel warm on the inside. I still sputtered when I drank it, but I had to admit that it helped.

Eugene struggled against the nasty tonic, but Pa made

him take it anyway. Pa even gave Eugene an extra spoonful for good measure.

Miss O'Neill gave us cups of hot water to drink. My numb hands and feet began to ache as feeling slowly returned.

"What happened?" I asked. "I remember pulling Eugene out of the pond and starting to walk back."

"Pa and George went looking for you two," said Ma, "and they saw you—with Eugene on your back—stumble out of the woods. When you fell, they raced to you. George carried Eugene back, and Pa carried you. Now, don't talk too much. You need rest."

After a good long while, I finally warmed up and was ready to shed the blankets. We were lucky that it wasn't any colder than it was.

The first thing that Mr. and Mrs. Dinwidden told Eugene was that they were displeased at how he had wandered off without telling them where he was going.

The first thing that Ma and Pa told me was that they were thankful that God had protected me and kept me safe. The different responses by Eugene's parents and my parents were never lost on me.

Eugene began sobbing. "He pushed me," said Eugene, pointing at me. "He pushed me in. He tried to drown me. He wanted to kill me."

Kate walked up to Eugene and slapped him in the face as hard as I've ever seen anyone slapped. "Eugene, I know Johnny, and he would never, ever do that. You apologize right now or you're going to get this," she said, holding up a fist.

"Kate!" shouted Pa. "Sit down right now. I want you to apologize to Eugene."

Kate looked down at the ground, but she didn't apologize.

"Kate, do it," ordered Pa again.

Kate looked up at Eugene and said, "I'm sorry for hitting you, Eugene." Then she sat down.

Pa looked at me and asked quietly, "Johnny, what happened?" I told him the whole story, just like it occurred. And Pa believed me with no hesitation. At that moment, I realized one thing. The reward of always telling the truth as you're growing up is that people will believe you when it really matters.

10
Corning

The morning met us with slightly warmer weather and a heavy rain that wouldn't have been so bad if it hadn't made the road so muddy. Because of the sloppy road conditions, we all began the day's journey riding in our respective wagons as we continued working our way toward Corning. That didn't last for long.

We came to the bottom of a hill that was steeper and longer than any hill we had encountered up to that point. Pa stopped the wagon, stepped out, and walked maybe halfway up the hill. He shook his head and started walking back down.

When he returned to the wagon, he said, "Okay, everybody out."

"Out? Why?" asked Mr. Dinwidden.

"We have a good-sized hill here," said Pa.

"And?" asked Mr. Dinwidden.

"Our wagons will never make it up this hill, in this mud, with all of us still in the wagons."

"Are you sure?"

"No, but getting out now and walking up is a whole lot easier than trying to get a stuck wagon unstuck. I'd rather not take the chance."

"Makes sense," said Mr. Dinwidden. "What do we need to do?"

"Well," said Pa, "we need to hitch up four horses on a wagon, pull the wagon up the hill, unhitch the team, and go back down the hill and get the next wagon. And then we'll do it again for the third wagon."

We all got out of the wagons—that is, everybody except for Mrs. Dinwidden and Eugene—and walked over to the side of the road while George and Elias began double-teaming the horses with the first wagon.

"Gene," she said, addressing her husband, "I am not getting out of this wagon and walking up a muddy hill. I am staying here, and nothing, absolutely nothing, will get me out of my wagon."

Eugene said, "Well, if Mother is not getting out, then I don't believe I will."

"Dorothy and Eugene," replied Mr. Dinwidden, "please be reasonable. Everyone else is walking up the hill."

"Gene, it just doesn't suit me," said Mrs. Dinwidden. "My clothes will get dirty, and my shoes will be ruined. I refuse to do this."

"Father, I believe Mother is right," said Eugene.

"Dorothy, my dear, I don't know if our wagon can make it up this hill with you in it."

"Gene! How dare you say such a thing."

"Dorothy, I'm not implying anything about your size. I don't think the wagon can make it up the hill with anybody in it, period, let alone with two people in it."

"And why exactly do you think that, Gene?"

"Because John said so."

"Well, he doesn't know about this wagon, then. Their own wagons may very well get stuck, but ours, never."

Mrs. Dinwidden was being entirely unreasonable, it seemed to me, and Mr. Dinwidden was stuck in a tough situation.

Out of earshot of Mrs. Dinwidden, Pa said under his breath, "Gene, let them ride the wagon. It's okay—even if they get stuck, it's okay."

Mr. Dinwidden walked back to Mrs. Dinwidden and his son. "Dorothy, Eugene, you can stay in the wagon." The decision was made, and Mrs. Dinwidden had a look of regal superiority on her face. Eugene looked quite pleased as well.

The rest of us trudged up the hill. It took a fair amount of work to double-team the horses on each wagon, but George and Elias were really the masters of this task. Strong, quick, and efficient, those two could rearrange horses almost as fast as you could say Abraham Lincoln.

With the four-horse team, Pa's wagon successfully climbed the hill, but just barely.

The Dinwidden's wagon, carrying Mrs. Dinwidden and Eugene, made it about one-quarter of the way up the hill before the wheels dug themselves into the mud and became solidly stuck.

Mr. Dinwidden walked back toward Mrs. Dinwidden with an I-told-you-so look, but Mrs. Dinwidden snapped at him, "You told me I could stay in the wagon, Gene. Now, I need you to carry me over to the side." The side of the road—where we had walked up the hill—wasn't nearly as muddy as the main part of the road that the wagons needed to use.

Mr. Dinwidden shrugged. "Dorothy, I can't carry you. I suggest you try walking to the side yourself." He didn't stay and wait for her response. He simply walked over to the side and waited.

Mrs. Dinwidden and Eugene sat in the wagon, glancing around as if they were hoping for someone to rescue them, someone to make a miracle happen.

Eugene frowned. "I told you we would get stuck, Father. We're never going to get out, not out of this deep mud. We'll be here the rest of the winter and we'll freeze to death."

"Eugene!" snapped an angry and annoyed Mr. Dinwidden. "We're all in this together, son. I know this will come as a shock, but the world does not revolve around you."

Eugene's cheeks turned beet red, either from embarrassment or anger.

"Dorothy," said Pa, calmly and in a soft voice, "the four horses cannot pull your wagon up the hill while you are in it. Two of the four horses are mine. I need my horses in order to continue our move west. I plan to keep going. I can go with or without your wagon. But if your wagon is coming with us, I really need for you to get out of the wagon and walk up the hill."

Fortunately, Mrs. Dinwidden had enough sense to realize that she and Eugene would have to walk up the hill just like everyone else had. Eugene climbed out of the wagon first, but instead of immediately walking to the side of the road—and getting out of the way—he stood there right next to the wagon, waiting for Mrs. Dinwidden. Holding her cane, Mrs. Dinwidden stepped one foot out of the wagon and onto the sloppy, soggy road. Unfortunately, her first step plunged deeper into the mud than she was expecting, and when she tried moving her other foot, she lost her grip on the wagon, and her cane went flying. Trying to keep her balance, she waved her arms in a flurry. She reminded me of a bird trying to dry itself off after playing in a puddle.

A look of horror appeared on Eugene's face. I think he foresaw the immediate future. "Mother, no, don't fall!" cried Eugene. But it was too late. Mrs. Dinwidden had lost her balance. As she was falling, in desperation she reached out to grab onto anything she could find. She found Eugene. With a SPLAT, they fell down into the muck, she landing on top of him.

Mrs. Dinwidden came up sputtering—she was covered top to bottom with the rich, black Iowa mud, some of which apparently had ended up in her mouth. After she managed to pull herself upright to standing position, she took a step toward the side of the road and then slipped and went down again. She was having a miserable time. Eugene was fairing no better.

Mrs. Dinwidden was fuming and—unlike Kate and me, who, I had to admit, were silently enjoying the spectacle—she obviously saw nothing funny in the situation. Eugene wasn't particularly pleased about it either.

Mr. Dinwidden looked at Mrs. Dinwidden and said, "Dorothy, it is tedious having to get out of the wagon each time we come to a big hill, I know. It's just one of the things we have to do, and if we want to get—"

"Gene," blurted Mrs. Dinwidden in a shrill voice, "be quiet!"

As Mrs. Dinwidden walked up the hill, I heard her grumbling about who put this hill here in the first place—she wasn't stupid enough to put a hill right there in the middle of the road, and why hadn't they simply chosen a route with flat roads to Nebraska instead—and why were they leaving Iowa anyway and why couldn't everyone be more civilized, and on and on.

While Mrs. Dinwidden and Eugene were wallowing in self-pity, Pa kept the rest of us focused on the task at hand.

"Gene," said Pa, "we've got to get that wagon the rest of the way up the hill. Looks like we might be getting a bit muddy. Let's all roll up our sleeves and go to work."

Every male in the party, except of course for Eugene, walked down to the mud-stuck wagon, ready to help. With George leading the four horses as they pulled the wagon, and with the rest of us pushing, pulling, and lifting, the wagon eventually started rolling forward. We slipped and struggled on the slippery slope, but after a lot of effort we finally had the wagon sitting at the top of the hill. Worn out and breathing hard, we all were covered with mud from head to toe.

George's wagon was next, and we were able to get it up the hill without much difficulty.

"We did it!" exclaimed Miss O'Neill. "We made it to the top of the hill!"

"Well, for those of us who had fun on this hill, take a look west," said Pa. We all turned and faced the road ahead of us. From the top of our hill, we could see that the road led to two more hills like the one we had just climbed.

"What are we waiting for?" asked Miss O'Neill. "Let's go!"

"I appreciate your enthusiasm, Lucy," said Pa, smiling. "A good attitude goes a long way on a trip like this."

Mrs. Dinwidden didn't say anything—other than at first sighing out-loud in resignation—as we assaulted the hills. She seemed to be deep in thought and pretty much just kept to herself.

When we all were at the top of the third hill for the day, we could see the town of Corning in the valley below, with a handful of small farms between us and the town. After descending the hill, Pa said, "Let's head into town."

"John! Absolutely not!" said Ma.

"Why not?"

"We can't go into town looking like this," she said. "We look disgusting!"

Pa knew enough not to respond.

Mrs. Dinwidden lifted up her head and glanced at us, and she seemed startled by our appearance, as though she were seeing us for the first time. "Oh my! You men are ... filthy!"

She bit her lip and looked down, as though she was waiting for Pa to scold her. Instead of being angry, Pa merely said, "Thanks, everyone. We made it up the hills. Whew, I hope we don't encounter too many more of those!"

For the longest time, no one said a word. Then, in a meek, little voice, Mrs. Dinwidden said, "I'm sorry."

There was a long moment of silence. I think maybe we were all stunned.

Clearing her throat and speaking louder this time, she repeated her words. "I'm sorry, I'm so sorry. Oh dear, how foolish of me," she sighed. "I apologize to everyone. From now on, I'm walking up all the hills."

Then she began chuckling. "If I am wearing even half the mud that you are wearing, I must be quite a sight ... like ... like one big, giant snow lady, only with mud—a mud lady!"

We heated pots of water on the little stove and began taking turns getting most of the dirt and mud off our skin. Mrs. Dinwidden was pleasant and talkative. Was God using these hills to change that woman? I didn't know if he was, but I knew that he could.

After we had finished getting all cleaned up and changed into dry clothing, Ott approached Pa. Breaking into song, Ott began:

> *We've had some luck*
> *I saw a good-sized buck*
> *A'standin' near the walnuts over there.*
>
> *A deer, oh dear,*
> *I've got a great idea'r*
> *My stomach sends a message loud and clear.*
>
> *I want to hunt*
> *I guess I'm rather blunt*
> *He'd make a nice big supper for us all.*

Pa surveyed the patch of walnut trees carefully. "I don't see anything, but you may very well be right."

Ott continued:

> *May I pursue*
> *And follow any clue*
> *Until I have some venison for us?*

Pa laughed and then responded with his own song:

> *Ott, take a horse*
> *Our Blackie take, of course*
> *I wish you luck with tracking down your foe.*

Elias, too
Should also ride with you
You'll find us somewhere farther down the road.

Pa cleared his throat and continued speaking. "I see a farmhouse around the corner up ahead. They might own the land. Go ask them for permission to hunt. I want to keep going, but you and Elias can catch up with us. We won't be too far past Corning. I think we'll eat dinner here before we move on."

"Come on, Elias!" said Ott. In a flash, Ott and Elias were on Blackie, trotting down the road to the farmhouse.

The rest of us began our dinner of dried beef, dried fruit, and some bread. Not more than ten minutes later, we were startled to see Blackie, carrying Elias, sprinting around the corner back toward us!

"Ma!" gasped Elias, out of breath. "There's a woman in the farmhouse and she said she's having a baby. She's alone and she needs help!"

11
Doctor Ma

Ma grabbed her small bag of medical supplies, said, "Elias, take me there," and the two of them took off like a shot, racing Blackie down the road and around the corner.

If anyone could help with delivering a baby, it was Ma. Ma had plenty of experience in assisting with births. Ma's father, Grandfather Elias Shideler, had been a physician, and Ma had learned from him.

The turn of events happened so quickly—one moment, Ma and Elias were there, and the next moment they were gone—that the rest of us were left speechless and befuddled.

"What do we do now, Pa?" asked Kate.

"I was going to ask you the same question, Kate," said Pa, laughing. "Well, okay … I think perhaps we should all go to the farmhouse around the bend and practice the fine art of being available to help out without being too much underfoot."

As we pulled into the farmyard about an hour later, Elias and Ott came running out to greet us. "Ma would like Miss O'Neill and Mrs. Dinwidden to go into the house," said Elias. "The rest of us are supposed to wait in the barn and stay out of the way."

Miss O'Neill and Mrs. Dinwidden went inside.

Moments later we heard a muffled scream, the cry of someone in pain, come from the house.

"Let's … uh … let's go in the barn," said Pa, motioning to the barn behind the house.

"Is something wrong, Pa?" Kate asked, almost on the verge of tears.

"I don't know, Kate. We should pray for her."

"I have been praying for her, Pa. You can pray with me if you want," said Kate.

Pa smiled. That was his little Kate.

Ott, patiently waiting through all of this, said, "Pa, is it okay with you if I go try to find that buck?"

"I'd like to go too," said Elias.

"And me too," echoed George.

"Sure, that's fine," said Pa. "You know where to find us."

The rest of us—Mr. Dinwidden, Pa, Eugene, Kate, and I—went in the barn.

I sat down in a corner, near Mr. Dinwidden. He looked at me with a slight smile and said, "It's scary, isn't it."

"Yes sir, it sure is."

"You know, John," he said, turning toward Pa, "this is how I lost my mother."

"Oh, I'm sorry."

"My mother was expecting, and she thought she was about a month away from having the baby. I was five years old. Father took a trip into town to the general store, and then he decided to stop in the saloon and play a card game or two. The card game or two turned into fifteen or twenty—a long time—and while he was gone,

Mother started delivering earlier than expected."

Mr. Dinwidden paused and took a deep breath. Pa was silent.

"Something went wrong—the baby wasn't coming out. I didn't know what to do. I remember … I remember Mother falling off to sleep. Father wasn't there. And she never woke up. She never …"

Mr. Dinwidden lowered his head.

"Gene, I'm sorry. That must have been so hard."

Mr. Dinwidden wiped his eyes. "My father and I never were close after that. I always blamed him for Mother's death. After I grew up, I left home and moved back east for a while. Father eventually changed his ways—they said he got religion and that he felt terrible for what he had done. I knew that God wanted me to forgive him, but it took me a long time to get to that point. I tried to avoid God. I stopped going to church. Finally, I came back out to visit Father. I intended to reconcile with him, but by the time I got there, he was dead. I didn't forgive him until it was too late."

Silence filled the barn.

Eugene was sulking in the corner of the barn. I really didn't feel like talking to him, but something inside of me directed me to walk over and sit next to him. I'm still not sure why I did it, but it was like my body went one way even though my mind was screaming, "No!"

"Eugene, what's wrong?" I asked.

"What's wrong? You're asking me what's wrong? I'll tell you what's wrong. We're just sitting here, waiting for a baby to be born to somebody we don't even know. We could be getting closer to Nebraska, but we're stuck here in this stinky barn."

"Eugene, we aren't stuck. We're here by choice, because we want to help out."

"Why can't someone else help? Why do we have to be the ones helping?"

"God brought us here at the right time. We have to be the ones—there is no one else."

"You think God brought us here? It was just because Ott wanted to go deer hunting. If he didn't want to hunt, none of this would have happened."

"Well, the baby would still be coming, either way. But we could be here to help or we could not be here to help. God chose us to be here. We can choose to accept or we can turn away."

"What happens if we turn away?" asked Eugene.

"Do you remember what happened to Jonah?"

"The whale guy?"

"Yes."

"Um, not really. I know he was swallowed by a whale."

"Well, God wanted him to go and preach to Nineveh, but Jonah was afraid of the people there. So, he turned and went in the opposite direction, hopping on a boat that was heading toward a place named Joppa. God got angry at Jonah. A storm came up and the men on the boat threw Jonah overboard. The fish swallowed him and spit him out onto shore three days later. Jonah decided it was better to follow God's command, so he went to Nineveh."

"There are no whales out here on the prairie, Johnny."

"I know that, Eugene. I don't know what would happen here if we disobeyed God's call. Maybe we'd get swallowed by a buffalo. I don't know, maybe nothing would happen. But I do know one thing."

"What's that?"

"Well, there's a good feeling you get when you help someone. Know what I mean?"

"Um, well, no, I guess not," he said. "That all sounds pretty silly to me."

"You know why? It's because you always think only of yourself. You've never thought of someone else's needs. You've never helped anyone!"

Eugene had nothing to say to that. Maybe what I said was mean. I wasn't trying to be mean, but I had lost my patience by that point. Anyway, I wanted to be honest and give Eugene something to think about.

Not long after that, the older boys returned from hunting, empty-handed. They hadn't seen any sign of the deer.

It was near dusk when we heard the cry of a baby, and we all hurried from the barn to the house. Mrs. Dinwidden met us at the front door. "Wait right here—don't come in." A few moments later, Ma came out, soaked in sweat and looking exhausted. She had a smile on her face.

"How is it?" asked Pa.

Ma took a deep breath. "The baby was breach, but we somehow got it turned around. I think everything is going to be okay," she said. "The Wilsons have a new baby daughter." Tears of joy welled up in her eyes.

"Hooray!" Kate yelled. "It's a girl!"

We all applauded and cheered.

"Shh!" Ma reprimanded us. "Mrs. Wilson needs to sleep."

At that moment, a man on a horse rode into the farm yard. He looked both startled and annoyed to find a host of strangers standing outside the house.

"Who are you, and where's Anna?" he asked.

"In the bedroom," replied Ma. "Are you Mr. Wilson?"

"Yes, Robert Wilson."

"Mr. Wilson, your wife and new baby are happy, healthy, and resting. They would love to see you."

A smile appeared on Mr. Wilson's face, and he rushed into the house.

"Well, I guess we should be going now," said Pa.

"Not yet, John. I think they might want some help. Let's wait a bit and see."

Mr. Wilson came to the door, carrying his new daughter. "Please, won't you just stay the night?" asked Mr. Wilson. "It's already dark. You may as well stay here, get a good night's sleep, and you can be off early in the morning."

"We don't want to impose—" said Pa.

"We would love to stay the night, Mr. Wilson, as long as we can take care of dinner," interrupted Ma, giving Pa a stern look. "I also want a turn at rocking the baby tonight so that the two of you can get some sleep."

Mr. Wilson went back in the bedroom to be with his wife, and Ma whispered to Pa, "It's to everybody's advantage."

"All right, Catherine. I will defer to your wisdom in this."

The three women slept in the house. The rest of us—we men and Kate—had a comfortable night sleeping on the straw in the barn.

By seven o'clock the next morning it was already forty-five degrees and the snow was melting. We set out as quickly as we could—the wagons were still packed from the night before, since we hadn't slept in them—and we were on the road by eight o'clock.

We reached Corning within an hour, at about the same time the rain started. Pa decided we should pass through town and continue to the next town, Villisca.

12
Villisca

The rain came down steadily, in torrents at times, making travel difficult that day on the soft, muddy way to Villisca. The road surface was like a thick, sticky paste that caked up on our boots and, more important, created problems for the wagon wheels.

Every few hundred feet, we stopped the wagons and scraped the mud off of the wheels. Then we would travel another few hundred feet and do it all over again. By the time we reached Villisca, we were ready for the day to be over. Wet and muddy, we were exhausted, and everyone was tired and grumpy—well, almost everyone.

Miss O'Neill rose to the occasion, and with a tremendous burst of energy, she said: "Now all of you, listen to me. You have worked very hard today. You have given herculean efforts to make this journey go safely and smoothly. Tonight, I want you all to rest and relax. I will prepare the fire, cook the meal, and clean afterward. And if you behave, I will even tell you a bed time story after we eat. You don't have to do anything except whatever personal cleaning you want to address—I won't wash your faces for you—and the only other thing I require is that you show up for supper. How's that sound?"

"Miss O'Neill, if you ran for the office of president, I would vote for you," laughed Pa.

"I can help," Ma chimed in.

"Thank you for your offer, Mrs. Stevens, but please let me do this. It's something I want to do."

Ma nodded her consent, and Miss O'Neill went to work. With surprising quickness, she darted to and fro, dicing, slicing, stirring, and mixing. Whatever she was making smelled delicious.

Our traveling party wasn't the only group who noticed the aromas coming from the fire. We heard howling off in the distance.

"Coyotes?" I asked.

"No, wolves," said Pa. "Put Old Jack up in the wagon when we go to sleep tonight. I don't want him on the wrong end of a lopsided fight with a wolf."

"Do you think they're close, Pa?"

"They aren't too close, but they may be tracking us, looking for an opportunity. We need to keep our eyes open."

"Supper's on," announced Miss O'Neill. She revealed a pot of stewed rabbits and fried potatoes, followed by a delectable butter cake. It was a simple, yet delicious, meal. As promised, she did all of the cleanup herself.

"Gather 'round, gather 'round," said Miss O'Neal in a soft but intense voice. We all complied with her request and found seats around the campfire.

"I have a story to tell you that might be scary for some. Whether it actually happened or not, I will leave that to you to decide. If, during the story, you notice that the person sitting next to you is shaking with fright, feel free to turn to that person and say, 'Ma, it will be all right,' or, 'Pa, you don't need to be frightened.' After all, it's just pretend ... or is it?"

She looked at us with wide eyes and a kind of eerie smile. "Are we ready?" she whispered. Without waiting for a response, she said, "Then let us begin."

Mr. Kilgore, an acquaintance of the Jones family, had been dead for three days, and his body was on display at the wake in his home, which happened to be nearby, not far from the woods where we are sitting right now.

The Jones family had a boy named Reuben. Now, Reuben was a smart kid—if you asked him, he would have said that he was a *very* smart kid—and Reuben felt that he deserved some things—let's call them treasures—more than some of his friends.

Reuben knew that very few people would come in to visit the deceased—the dead person, Mr. Kilgore—because the old man never had many friends. Reuben also knew that Mr. Kilgore was very wealthy, possibly the richest man in the county.

"Father, can we go to Mr. Kilgore's wake?" asked Reuben of his father.

"Why, yes, I suppose so," he replied, and so the two of them went to the wake.

As Reuben had hoped, there were very few people at the wake. When Reuben walked up to the body, he noticed the beautiful rings on Mr. Kilgore's hands. The first thought that appeared in Reuben's mind was, *I must have one of those rings.*

Reuben waited for the opportune time, and then when he knew that nobody was looking, he actually reached out and pulled off a ring from one of Mr. Kilgore's fingers and put it in his pocket!

Well, at the supper table that night, three days after Mr. Kilgore had died, an argument started up amongst the Jones children. "That old codger was the best left-handed rock-thrower I've ever seen," said Fritz, one of the Jones boys. "Mr. Kilgore? He wasn't left-handed," said Reuben. "He was right-handed, sure as shootin'."

The argument with the two boys—Fritz and Reuben— became more heated, and finally the father, tired of all the bickering, said, "Look, why don't you two boys go over and look for yourself. The wake is still going on and the body is out there in the open."

The boys thought for a moment, and then one of them said, "But Father, how will we know just by looking at him whether he was right-handed or left-handed?"

The father said, "Well, think about it. If he were left-handed, wouldn't you expect to find more callouses on the left hand than the right? And if right-handed, then you'd find more callouses on the right than on the left."

The boys agreed that was a good way to find out, so off they went. They got to the house and knocked, but no one answered the door. The boys walked around the corner of the house and peeked in the window. The light was on and the body was plainly visible, alone, lying in the room on the funeral bier.

"Let's try knocking one more time," said Reuben.

"I think we should go home," said Fritz.

"We will, if no one answers this time."

So, they knocked a bit harder, and suddenly the door started swinging open. Of course, it creaked.

"Let's just get this over with," said Fritz. The boys walked into the parlor. The body was gone!

"Where's the body?" gasped Fritz.

Then they heard a sound in the kitchen. There was a heavy footstep, and then another, and then another.

"Who ... who's there?" asked Reuben in a shaky voice.

A slow, stale, musty, old voice answered, "You have my ring. I want my ring."

"Let's get out of here!" shouted Fritz, and the two boys ran out of the house, across the field, and down the path through the woods to their family.

The boys didn't tell their parents what they had seen, and that night the family went to bed in their house as usual.

Fritz awoke with a start when he heard a low, stale, musty, old voice whisper, "Where's my ring? I want my ring." He sat up in bed and heard the sounds of a whistling wind. *Oh, I must have been dreaming*, he thought to himself, and he fell back asleep.

He awoke again when he heard the sound of slow, heavy footsteps on the wood floor. He sat up in bed and heard a loose, wood shutter banging against the front of the house. Again, he thought to himself that he was dreaming. And he fell back asleep.

He awoke a third time when he heard Reuben's scream. Fritz jumped out of bed, lit a candle, and ran down the hall to Reuben's room. The door was ajar. Fritz peeked into the room. Reuben's bed was empty. His sheets were stained with blood. His bedroom window was wide open, the curtains blowing wildly in the wind.

And Reuben was never seen again. The end.

I glanced over at Eugene. He looked about as white as the belly of a catfish that had never seen daylight, and he was shaking. I wasn't sure what had gotten into him, but he didn't look well.

After most everyone had gone to bed, Pa and I were sitting at the campfire, talking.

"Johnny, is something bothering you?"

"Pa," I said softly, "why did you agree to let the Dinwiddens come along with us?"

Pa smiled. "I don't rightly know, Johnny."

I didn't want to argue with Pa, but I felt that I should set him straight on a couple of points.

"Pa, Eugene has caused so much trouble, and we aren't even halfway to where we're going. And they're slowing us down." There, I said it.

"I know it doesn't make sense to us, but somehow I

think it makes sense to God," said Pa.

"What do you mean, Pa?"

"You know how when you're lost or don't know what to do, and you're looking for a sign … suppose for example that you are lost in the woods and you see tracks in the snow … what are you going to do?" asked Pa.

"Well, I suppose you're going to follow the tracks."

"Right. And I believe that God sometimes gives us clear tracks to follow. Before we left Polk City—the day that Mr. Dinwidden came to see us—in my mind I saw tracks in the snow. I didn't know why I saw them, and I wasn't sure where they would lead us, but I knew that God was showing me what I should do, plain as day."

"Did you hear his voice?"

"Whose voice—God's?"

"Yes."

"Well Johnny, I didn't hear an actual sound, but even though my mind was telling me that this would be crazy, something deep down in my heart told me that it's the right thing to do. It was as clear to me as seeing tracks in the snow."

I sat there thinking for a minute or two.

"Pa?"

"Yes, Johnny."

"Does God show you these tracks every time that you don't know what to do?"

"I don't think so … but often it seems that when I have to make a hard decision, or when it seems God wants me to do something that others might think nonsense, I get this feeling inside that I know what he wants me to do."

"Pa, what happens when things are hard but you don't see any tracks in the snow?"

"Those are the best times, Johnny."

"Why's that, Pa?"

"When you don't see tracks ahead of you, it can only mean one thing?"

"What?"

"If he's not walking ahead of you, then he's walking *with* you."

I thought about that some more as I was falling asleep that night. I was glad God was walking with me, because I could hear the wolves again, howling in the distance.

13
Clarinda

I had a fitful sleep that night and woke up exhausted the next morning. Dreams of wolves filled my head, and I kept thinking about the spooky story that Miss O'Neill told us around the campfire.

I was sitting on a log, drinking a cup of hot water to warm myself up, when Pa asked me to go fetch a few more pieces of firewood. When I finished, I returned to my seat on the log. There, lying on the log where I had been sitting, was my button! I picked it up. It was still warm, and the string was dry.

"Hey," I shouted, "I found my button. Does anybody know where this came from?" No one claimed to know anything about the button, but everyone seemed happy that I had found it, even Eugene.

"Eugene, do you know about this?" I asked.

"Um … no, Johnny. Maybe it was in your pocket— yeah, that's it, maybe it's been in your pocket the whole time, and it accidentally fell out this morning and, well, here it is."

"Not likely," I said.

"Well … um … I'm happy you have your button back," said Eugene.

I couldn't argue with that. "I am too," I said.

As we began the journey to the town of Clarinda, Iowa, the weather was a little cooler, but the roads were still wet and muddy. We slogged along, stopping frequently to clean the wagon wheels, and we had another hill that required us to unload all the passengers from the wagons so that the wagons could make it up the muddy incline.

Miss O'Neill was walking beside me at one point. "Johnny, I'm glad you found your button," she said.

"Well, thank you, Miss O'Neill, for the use of your white horse," I laughed. "I guess it helped."

"I suppose it did," she said with a wink.

All in all, we made good progress and, with a little bit of daylight remaining, we reached a place to set up camp just outside of Clarinda. We had gone maybe sixteen miles.

We saw no other travelers on the road that day, though I hadn't realized it until Pa mentioned it at supper.

"With the roads so sparsely populated—that is, there aren't many other travelers around—we all need to be on our toes for anything that looks suspicious."

"What do you mean, Pa?" asked Kate.

"He means that we're good targets for a hold-up," said Elias, cutting right to the core.

"But Pa, what will we do if outlaws come?" asked Kate, with a worried look.

"We'll do what we should do. We'll stay calm, try not to panic, and say silent prayers."

"I hope we don't have to do that though," said Kate.

"Me too," said Pa. "Me too."

The whinnying and neighing of horses, followed by

a shotgun blast, woke me up. I heard George shout, "Wolves!"

The camp was instantly besieged with the snarling, screaming shrieks of a pack of wolves. I looked out a crack in the sideboard. It was too dark to see anything clearly, but it sounded like the horses had panicked and were bucking, trying to break free from their tethers.

Old Jack was frantic, barking and trying to climb out of the bottom berth.

"John!" screamed Ma. I heard a crash against the sideboard and then a loud CRACK—the sound of a stick or a rifle landing on a wolf's head.

BLAST! Pa's gun fired, and something fell to the ground with a thud. I was hoping it was a wolf.

Then I heard two more gun reports as Elias and George fired their rifles.

The howling, raucous cries of the wolves continued, though not as intense as before.

"Old Jack!" Pa shouted. "Where's Old Jack?"

"He's okay, Pa. He's in here with me," I said.

"No! Get away!" yelled Mr. Dinwidden. Their wagon was being attacked too!

"They need help!" said Pa, referring to the Dinwiddens. He jumped out of our wagon and ran toward theirs.

"John!" cried Ma.

George, apparently hearing Pa, jumped into the fray.

Pa kicked one wolf away from the Dinwidden's wagon and shot it, killing it instantly. George was pulled down to the ground by two wolves. Pa couldn't shoot them without shooting George too, so he threw down his gun, drew his knife, and dived onto one of the wolves, knocking it off of George. The wolf escaped Pa's grasp and turned on him, clamping its teeth into his arm, but Pa drove the knife into the wolf's chest, killing it. George, meanwhile, stabbed and killed the other wolf. Then Pa somehow managed to pull another wolf off of the Dinwiddens' wagon, shooting and stabbing it.

There was one more blast, and I heard Elias say, "Got it!"

Pa called out, "See any more?"

"No sir," said Elias. "I think we got at least seven or eight, and we probably scared the others away."

"George!" shouted Pa. George was lying on the ground, next to the wagon. "George, how bad are you hurt?"

"My legs, Pa … my right leg … it hurts. It really hurts."

Ma jumped out of the wagon and ran to George, leaning over him to try to examine him in the dark.

"Johnny, Kate, bring the lanterns," ordered Ma. When we reached her with the lanterns she lit them.

"George!" gasped Kate. "Ma, is he going to be all right?"

"Yes, I believe he is," whispered Ma. "He is losing a lot of blood, though. Kate, go get some clean cloth from the wagon. We need to bind up his wounds immediately to stop the bleeding." Ma turned and looked at Pa. "John, how bad are you hurt?"

Pa looked at his arms. "Just my left arm, nothing that a bandage or two can't handle."

"I need a knife or shears," said Ma, turning back to George.

"Here, Ma," said Elias, pulling out his knife and handing it to her.

Without saying another word, Ma cut George's trousers above the wounds and then carefully peeled away the material, exposing the torn flesh. George's leg looked bad.

Kate returned with the cloth. Ma tore the cloth into strips, and Ma and Miss O'Neill began dressing George's torn flesh.

"Johnny, Kate, or anyone … I need a fire. I need two pots of hot water," said Ma.

"Two?" asked Kate.

"Yes, one pot will be for washing the wounds. Put a piece of dried beef in the other pot and we will make beef broth for George and your father. That will help their strength return."

When they finished with George's leg, Ma said, "Lucy, if you will take care of George's arm, I'll tend to John."

Miss O'Neill removed George's shirt and gasped. His shoulder had several deep gashes.

"Catherine, I will need your guidance on what to do with this shoulder," whispered Miss O'Neill. "He's hurt pretty bad."

"Lucy, just wrap it tightly for now. When we get the hot water we can clean the wound before fully dressing it."

Pa removed his shirt. Under normal circumstances, his arm wounds might have elicited a more concerned response from Ma. However, his arm didn't look to be nearly as bad as George's injuries.

"Oh, this isn't too bad," said Ma.

Pa smiled. Of course his arm hurt, and he knew that Ma knew that it hurt, but he also knew that Ma meant that he was not as bad off as George.

The Dinwidden family—all three of them—walked up to Pa.

"John, thank you for coming to the aid of our wagon," said Mr. Dinwidden.

"Yes, thank you," said Mrs. Dinwidden. "We are … we are very grateful."

Eugene didn't say anything. He didn't even look at Pa.

Pa simply nodded in silence.

After two pots of water had been sufficiently heated on the fire, Ma and Miss O'Neill began washing and redressing all of the wounds. George winced as the hot water cleansed the gashes in his leg and arm.

"I'm … dizzy," he said in a barely audible voice. "Ow, my leg. My leg hurts … what … what happened?"

"Shh," said Ma. "We can talk about that later. Everything's okay, and you're going to be fine. Here, drink this. It'll make you strong." She lifted a cup of hot broth to his lips.

After Pa and George had gone to lie down and the rest

of us were sitting by the fire, waiting for our hearts to calm down from all the excitement, Ott stuck his head out of the back wagon. "Hey!" he shouted. "What's going on? Why is everybody up in the middle of the night? Did I miss anything?"

Ma shook her head and sighed.

14
Shenandoah

Georderge is weak from losing so much blood last night," said Ma, "and I've done about all I know how to do. We need to get him to a doctor. John, are you able to drive the wagon?"

Ma was tired and weary—we were all tired and weary—from the harrowing events of the previous night. Ott and I, trying to be helpful, had already set up the little stove because we guessed that we wouldn't have time for a campfire to cook breakfast. George was conscious but looked like ... well, he looked like he had been attacked by a couple of mean, hungry wolves.

"I don't think I should try to drive today, so Ott will take the reins of this wagon and Elias the third wagon," said Pa. "We'll put George in our wagon so that you can keep an eye on him and me both. We should get going soon. A storm is coming in." He pointed to the west where dark, ominous clouds loomed overhead.

"What's the nearest town?" asked Ma.

"Shenandoah."

"Can we make it there today?"

"Maybe, but it depends on the weather," said Pa.

"Well then, let's get going. Johnny and Ott, put away the

little stove and pull out some cold food—carrots, cheese, and dried beef—from the provision box. We'll eat on the way. Elias, help me put George in our wagon. Kate, check the camp site and make sure we have everything."

And so we set out toward Shenandoah, Iowa, getting closer and closer to the Missouri River.

The snow started up again, and by sunset the strong wind and thick snow forced us to stop for the day. Pa guessed that we were still a good three or four miles from Shenandoah. The temperature was dropping quickly, and Pa said we should choose the safer option of settling in for the night instead of getting lost in the snow storm.

During the night the wind calmed down, but the snow continued to fall. We awoke with another four inches of powder on top of everything. Without the brutal wind, though, it was bearable.

Ott and I were the first two up that morning. We were gathering snow in buckets to replenish our fresh water supply when we heard the sound of hooves trotting on the road. I looked, and sure enough, coming down the road was a man wearing a deerskin jacket and riding a coal-black mare.

I also heard the cocking of a rifle, raised and ready to go. Elias was prepared, just in case.

"Good mornin'," said the man to Ott and me as the horse slowed to a halt.

"Morning," responded Ott, nodding cautiously.

"Looks like you survived last night's snow well enough," the man said.

"Well enough," said Ott, wary and deliberate as he tried to determine whether he trusted the man who had just entered our camp.

"Yep, last night was cold and snowy, but there wasn't much wind. But take a look west and see what's comin'," said the stranger, turning and pointing in that direction. "See them black clouds? That's serious."

Ott and I looked west. Some distance away, a line of black clouds blanketed the horizon, so dark and so distinct that it looked like a curtain hanging in the sky, separating night from day.

"You didn't stop here just to chat about the weather," stated Ott.

"You're right about that, young man," he replied. "Two outlaws have been seen in this part of the state—they go by the names of James and Seth—and I was wondering if you'd seen them or anyone else suspicious. By the way, my name is Benson," said the man.

"Thank you for the information, Mr. Benson," said Pa, appearing from behind the lead wagon. "We will keep our eyes open for any suspicious-looking people. Can you tell me how far we are from Shenandoah? We have to get our oldest boy to a doctor. A pack of wolves attacked us a couple of nights back, and my boy's leg and shoulder are injured."

The man stiffened and a shadow seemed to settle on his face, as though a memory came back to haunt him. "I am so sorry to hear about your son, Mr. …"

"Stevens," replied Pa.

It would have been obvious to anyone seeing Pa that he was injured and in need of medical care.

"I am pleased to meet you, Mr. Stevens," said Mr. Benson. He sat on his horse in silence for a few moments and then said, "Listen, Mr. Stevens, I have a proposition for you."

We all looked at Mr. Benson with curiosity. What was he going to offer?

"We've got a big storm headed our way, folks. Dealing with snow is one thing, but a winter fury like the one approaching can be deadly. Our farmhouse is just over two miles down the road, on the edge of Shenandoah. Our local doctor is in town, just about a half-mile past our place. My wife and I would be honored if you would come stay with us for a day or two until the weather clears. I can take your son to see Doc. Looks like you might need to see him, too."

"Oh, I think we'll be all right," said Pa. "We've survived the trip so far, and—"

"Mr. Stevens, I insist—not because I'm trying to pass myself off as the good Samaritan, but because it's the right thing to do. You've got a son who requires medical attention. It wouldn't be good to be out in a winter storm."

"Well, okay," began Pa, "I'm sure none of us would object to warming up and coming in out of the cold for a spell. We've got plenty of our own food, but we don't have good control of the weather yet."

We loaded the wagons and went on down the road about two miles, turning off into a well-kept farm. The Bensons had a large barn. We pulled the wagons up to the side of the barn to protect them from the wind, and after we unhitched the horses and took them into the barn for shelter, Mr. Benson invited us into the farmhouse and introduced us to his wife.

While Mr. Benson took George and Pa to the doctor in town, Mrs. Benson prepared a delicious breakfast of eggs, sausages, biscuits with homemade grape preserves, and steaming hot coffee.

Even Eugene was grateful for the opportunity to sit inside, out of the snowy wind, and eat a wonderful breakfast. I looked over at him at one point. He was diving into his food like a starving dog in a pile of soup bones.

This fact wasn't lost on Mrs. Benson. "Eugene, you look like you haven't eaten for a year!"

Eugene looked up, cheeks bulging with a biscuit he was devouring. His face was flushed. He was embarrassed.

"The foob ib goob," is what I heard him say.

"Eugene," said Mrs. Dinwidden, "please don't speak with your mouth full!"

Eugene swallowed. "This food is good, Mrs. Benson," he repeated, this time understandably.

He glanced over at me. I smiled and nodded. He nodded and returned what looked like an attempt at a smile. I wasn't sure, not having ever seen him smile before.

Shortly before noon, Mr. Benson and Pa walked in the door.

"Pa!" cried Kate with glee. "You're back!" Then she tried to look behind Pa. "Where's George?"

"George is in the wagon. Elias, come help me bring him in. He can't walk on his own right now." Pa took a deep breath. "George has a fever, but the doctor washed the wounds again and applied some kind of poultice, and he thinks George will be just fine. He just needs bed rest."

"How about you, John? Did he look at your arm?"

"Yes, Catherine, and he said I'll be fine and that I just need time to let it heal."

Ma walked up to Pa and gave him a hug, one of the rare times I had seen them show affection in front of everybody.

Pa went back outside with Elias and they brought

George inside. George's face was an ashen color, accented by his sunken cheeks, but he was awake. Mrs. Benson put George to bed in a small room in the back of the house—she said it was an office of some kind—and she shut the door so that George could sleep.

It turned out it was a good thing that we stopped at the Benson's farm, because the storm came in with a vengeance that afternoon. For a while, we couldn't even see the barn from the house.

The farm house was pretty noisy with all of us there. Not that it was a small house, but our traveling party added eleven people, and I don't think there's a house anywhere that could take eleven more people and still keep on the quiet side.

At one point I realized I hadn't seen Eugene for a couple of hours; nor had I seen Mr. Benson. I mentioned it to Mrs. Benson, and she said, "Some chores don't stop just on account of the weather. My husband took Eugene out to the barn to have him help milk the cow."

The storm kept howling and the snow was drifting up against the barn and the house. This was as bad as any storm I had seen before.

A little bit later, both Eugene and Mr. Benson came in through the inside porch at the back of the house—they called it a mud room—where we had put our snow-covered coats and boots when we first arrived.

"Hi, Eugene," I said.

"Johnny, guess what? I milked a cow this afternoon! That's my first time!" Eugene was smiling a genuine smile.

Pa walked into the mud room at that moment. "Who wants to go with me to check on the animals?" he asked.

Eugene spoke up. "It's done, Mr. Stevens. I went out

with Mr. Benson to milk the cow, and we made sure all the other animals had food and water."

"Well, Eugene, Mr. Benson, thank you for doing that. I do still want to go out and check on the wagons. Johnny, get your coat and come with me."

"I tied a rope from the back door to the barn. Just hang on to the rope and you should be fine," said Mr. Benson.

Stringing ropes across a farmyard was common practice in the Midwest. Those midwestern snow storms were sometimes so bad that you couldn't see a thing, and it was easy to get turned around and confused.

Pa and I put on our boots and coats in the mud room. Pa opened the door and found the rope, and together we made our way through the snow. It was still blowing hard—it stung my cheeks and eyes—but we made it to the barn. Inside, the wind was whistling and it was brutally cold, but the animals seemed to be doing okay. Pa checked each of the wagon wheels to make sure they were not cracked and in need of repair.

Pa sat down in the straw and Old Jack lay across his lap. Pa motioned for me to sit down next to him, and he began stroking Old Jack underneath his neck and behind the ears, something that the dog really liked.

"Johnny, have you noticed anything unusual today?"

"You mean besides this snow storm?"

"Right."

"Well, Pa, Eugene hasn't been whining or griping about anything today. I even saw him smiling a couple times."

Pa nodded. "Ma said she noticed his smile at breakfast."

"And I think that usually he would be whining about not being able to go outside, or whining about having to go outside, or finding something to complain about. He hasn't complained since we've been here."

"You hit it right on the head, Johnny. I think Eugene is growing up a bit."

"Do you think we can convince him to go out in this storm and bring in some firewood from the woodpile?"

Pa laughed. "Don't try to make him change too much at once, Johnny. But if he's really started in the right direction, that's a good sign that he might turn out all right after all."

I smiled. "That would be nice, Pa."

"Yes, indeed," he agreed.

The wind was still howling as we made our way back to the farmhouse, but it wasn't quite as fierce as before. The storm seemed to be loosening up.

We awoke the next morning to crisp blue skies. It was cold—the thermometer outside the kitchen window said it was ten degrees—but the snow and wind had both stopped. I threw on my clothes quickly and went downstairs to see if I could help with chores.

As I walked into the mud room, the back door opened and Mr. Benson came in from outside. His cheeks were red.

"Mr. Benson, can I get some firewood for you?" I asked, hopeful that he had not already done all the work.

"Somebody already beat you to the punch," he said with a grin.

The door opened again and in stepped Eugene, carrying an arm-load of wood.

"Eugene!" I said in amazement.

"Good morning, Johnny," Eugene said with a smile.

"Eugene, how … I mean, did you get all that wood?"

"I only got some of it. Mr. Benson got most of it."

"Don't listen to him, Johnny. Eugene got half of it, at least."

"I'll have to admit it's cold out," said Eugene.

Mr. Benson added, "We would have stayed out longer if Eugene had his druthers. He wanted to bring in more, but I told him we needed to come inside and warm up some."

"I'll go feed the animals," I said, reaching for my boots.

"Oh, I did that," said Eugene.

"All the horses and Old Jack?"

"Done. And I played with Old Jack a while."

"Eugene, what time did you get up?"

"I'm not sure, but it was still dark outside."

"Well, I got up at 5:30," said Mr. Benson, "and Eugene was already up by then."

I whistled. Eugene wasn't just changing. He was a completely different person.

"Eugene, if you don't mind me saying so, you're not acting like you usually act."

"Johnny, it's going to be different now. But I don't want to talk about it right yet. I'm still thinking about things."

"Okay Eugene, fine by me."

"Friends?" asked Eugene, holding out his hand.

"Friends, Eugene," I said, taking his hand and shaking it.

Ma announced that morning that George's fever had broken and he was recovering. Mr. Benson suggested to Pa that we stay at least another day. Pa agreed.

We spent the rest of the day digging and shoveling a path through the snow drifts so that we'd be able to leave the next morning. Mrs. Benson kept us warm with a seemingly endless supply of hot cocoa and coffee. Eugene was acting a whole lot more like a plain ordinary person who didn't require extra numbers after his name. That made life happier for all of us.

As I lay in bed that night, I thought about how nice the Bensons had been to us. I also knew, though, that there were people in this world who weren't nice. I was soon to find that out, first hand.

15
Sidney

We passed through Shenandoah and headed down the road toward Sidney, hoping to get there by sundown. Not only was our load heavier—Mrs. Benson had given us a gallon of fresh milk, a couple pounds of butter, and a quart of honey—but each of us had gained a pound or two on account of Mrs. Benson's cooking!

We reached the outskirts of Sidney late in the day, when afternoon shadows were growing long. Pa sent Elias and Ott out hunting for game while the rest of us set up camp. Soon we had a fire going, and Ma put a pot of water on the fire, just waiting for the boys to return with some meat— we were hoping for rabbit or squirrel—to add to it. The wind was blowing from west to east, which is probably why we didn't hear the two men on horses who suddenly entered our camp.

It was apparent they were going to stop and not just pass us by. Old Jack started barking. It wasn't like him to bark if we were awake, unless he really felt uneasy. I could tell by the expression on Pa's face that he was a bit uneasy too.

One of the men dismounted and walked toward Pa.

"Well, what do we got here? Looks like a family or two is goin' somewhere. Ain't I right?"

"What's it to you, stranger?" asked Pa.

"Stranger? I know these parts better'n you, mister. I'd say you're the stranger around here, and it seems like it might be good for you to have a hired hand or two," he said, motioning to his partner, "to help protect your valuables."

The man who had gotten off his horse and was doing the talking was wearing a black hat and was in a brown jacket and black pants. The man on the horse, wearing a brown hat, blue dungarees, and a black jacket, was heavy-set with a mustache and beard.

"We have nothing of value with us," said Pa.

"I don't believe you," said the man. "You don't look rich, but you don't look poor neither. Show me what you got, and I'll tell you how much it'll cost you to protect it. There's outlaws that travel the country roads, and you can't be too careful these days. Ain't that right, Seth?"

"You got that right, James," said the other man as he climbed down off of his horse.

"Now, how about givin' me the pleasure of beholdin' all your treasure," said the man in the black hat, whose name apparently was James.

"Look mister, we're just a group of poor farmers head-ing out west so we can scratch out a living," said Pa.

"Well, you look here yourself, mister," retorted the man. "Seth and I are just poor cowboys who are trying to scratch out our own livin.'"

"Robbing from others is not scratching out a living," argued Pa.

"Who said anything about anybody being robbed? Seth,

did I say anything about anybody doin' any robbin'?"

"No James, you ain't said nothin' at all about robbin.'"

"That's right, Seth. All I told this gentleman was that we're available for hire to protect his valuables and all that he holds near and dear to his heart. And if you know what's good for you," he continued, looking at Pa, "you'll hire us."

"I told you, we have nothing," said Pa.

The one named James walked over to the fire, glanced in the pot, and said, "Your soup is a little thin." He kicked the pot off the fire, sending water everywhere.

I was pretty worried by this time. Pa was staying remarkably calm though. Some of it might have had to do with the fact that Pa had fought in the war. He had stared down the wrong end of a rifle before. I also suspected that he was feeling the peace that the Bible tells us comes from God, not from circumstances.

Pa continued. "Where are you from?"

"Missouri," said Seth.

"Hush up, Seth," said James. "Don't be tellin' no one our business."

"Missouri? Ever been to Kansas City?" asked Pa.

"Why, Kansas City, that's where my mama done borne and raised me," said Seth, smiling.

"Seth! Be quiet!" shouted James.

I saw Pa take a quick glance toward the thicket behind the wagons. It finally occurred to me that Pa was stalling, trying to prolong the discussion in case our hunters—Ott and Elias—made it back and could rescue us.

"Gentlemen, can't we just sit down and talk this through?" asked Pa, still looking remarkably calm.

"Listen, I've had enough," retorted James. He reached

in his jacket and pulled out a pistol.

"You know that you're not going to get away with this," said Pa softly.

"We got away with it last night," said Seth. "In fact, it worked twice."

"Shut up, Seth!" shouted James.

Pa jumped in and said, "Oh, you might rob us of all we have—which isn't much—and you might escape from the law, but there's somebody you can't escape from, somebody who's going to someday hold you accountable."

"Listen to the preacher, Seth. I think he's gonna want to baptize us in a moment."

"That might be tough, James," said Seth. "All the ponds are frozen over. Maybe they do ice-baptizin' like we do ice-fishin'." He laughed briefly at his own humor.

BANG!

The gun flew out of James' hand, and James doubled over, grimacing in pain.

BANG! BANG!

Snow and ice flew just inches from where James and Seth were standing.

"Let's go, James," shouted Seth, turning to run back to his horse.

WHACK!

As quick as lightning, a stout cane came down and clobbered Seth on the head. Mrs. Dinwidden was on the other end of the stick. Seth let out a gasp and stumbled, but both outlaws managed to make it to their horses, and they thundered off across the field and disappeared into the woods.

Elias and Ott stepped out from behind a wagon, where they had sneaked up after coming back from hunting.

Not moments later, we heard the thundering of hooves approaching us from the west.

Four riders soon came into view, each carrying a gun. One of them wore a badge.

"Evening," said the man with the badge, tipping his hat.

"Evening," said Pa.

"We're from Alexandria, just down the road a stretch. We've been tracking a couple of outlaws that go by the names of James and Seth, and we heard gunshots. You folks okay?"

"Yes sir. We just met James and Seth. In fact, they were here trying to get us to hire them to take care of our valuables."

"What about the gunshots?" asked the man.

"My boys had been out huntin', and they came back and surprised those two fellas with a little nifty shooting. That scared them off. They went down into those woods," Pa replied, pointing the direction they had gone.

"Much obliged," said the man, tipping his hat, "and Godspeed." Then to his horse he yelled, "HEEYAH!" and took off across the field, headed toward the woods. The others followed.

"Let's get out of here," said Pa. "Those two outlaws may be coming back." He paused a moment and then said, "Nice shooting, boys. Nice shooting."

Elias nodded and said, "Sorry we didn't bring home anything for dinner."

Pa smiled and said, "You boys did just fine."

I asked Pa if we should leave the main road and take less traveled roads, hoping to avoid the outlaws. Pa said the back roads were too isolated, that we might not see any other travelers, and that it was safer on the main road. That made sense to me.

We didn't go far—just the other side of Sidney— because daylight was fading. We kept lookout the entire time—Pa, Elias, Ott, and George all had their rifles ready. Though the Dinwiddens didn't have any guns, Mrs. Dinwidden had demonstrated her agility with a cane. We had no further incidents that night.

16
Mighty Missouri

After a quick, early breakfast, we were off to face the river. We headed a bit south and west, and by ten o'clock we were at the ferry landing near Alexandria, Iowa, just across the river from Nebraska City, Nebraska.

In front of us lay the Missouri River—broad, fast, and formidable—roaring on by, a worthy barrier with a thunderous voice issuing a challenge: "If you want to become Nebraskans, first you have to get past me."

My heart sank when I saw the long line of wagons waiting to get across the river. We didn't really have a choice in the matter, so we got in line and waited.

An official-looking man with a scowl on his face approached us.

"Ain't gonna happen," he said gruffly.

"Pardon?" said Pa.

"Ain't gonna happen this morning," said the man. "It'll be late afternoon at the earliest. That's the soonest I can get you across," he said, almost defensively.

"That's fine," said Pa.

"That's fine?" asked the man.

"Yes, that's fine. There are a lot of people who want to

cross the Missouri, and we'll take our turn. We will wait until you are ready to take us across."

"You aren't complaining?"

"Why should I complain?"

"Everyone else around here is complaining, and I figured you would too."

"Ain't gonna happen," said Pa, smiling.

The man's scowl disappeared, replaced with a smile.

"Sawyer is my name, Marvin Sawyer," he said.

"Stevens, John Stevens," said Pa, "from Polk City."

"I am the manager here," said Mr. Sawyer, "and I am the enforcer of the regulations. I didn't write the regulations, but I make sure we follow them. You cross the river in the order you arrived here, no exceptions."

"Makes sense," said Pa. "It would be chaos otherwise."

"Well, you would be surprised how many people ask to move up in the line, ahead of others who are in front of them. I hear all kinds of excuses."

"You're pretty busy for this time of year."

"Well, we're the northernmost ferry that is running, what with the snow and ice further north, so all customers from here northward who need ferry service get funneled to us."

No one came in behind us for a good while, so Pa and Mr. Sawyer had some time to chat. I didn't hear everything that was said, but Pa got Mr. Sawyer to laughing, and for a few minutes he looked like a happy man.

Then somebody walked up to Mr. Sawyer, complaining about something or other, and the frown returned.

Besides the two ferry boats that were hauling the wagons across the river, there was a larger boat that took train cars back and forth. The train would back a few cars onto the boat, where they would be unhooked. The train would pull forward, and then it would back up on another track and put more train cars next to the first cars. The boat would take the cars across, where another engine would pull the cars off the boat, one bunch at a time. I never thought about it before, how the trains could get across the rivers where there were no bridges, and I found it pretty interesting.

As we were milling about, I could still hear people grumbling and complaining around me.

"Pa?"

"Yes Johnny?"

"You know the part in the Bible where it talks about how the first shall be last and the last shall be first?"

"Yes, I know that part."

"Well, it seems that people forget that part sometimes."

"You're right, Johnny. And I think some people never learn it in the first place."

The mid-day sky was beautiful—perfect for moving. Even so, all around us people were complaining about the slowness of the ferry or the unfairness of the whole process, and we heard all kinds of reasons as to why this wagon or that wagon should be allowed to go next.

Shortly after noon, before we had dinner, Mr. Sawyer walked over. "Good afternoon, Mr. Stevens."

"Good afternoon, Mr. Sawyer," said Pa. "Care to join us for dinner? We'll be eating sometime in the next hour."

"Thanks, but I won't be able to join you for dinner. Mr. Stevens, I appreciate your patience. Frankly, everyone else around here is complaining except for your group. People like you make my job a whole lot easier."

Later that afternoon, Mr. Sawyer came to Pa and said it

was our turn to go. Pa shook Mr. Sawyer's hand and we all took our places with the wagons. Within minutes we were on board the ferry, along with seven or eight other wagons, and we were crossing the mighty Missouri!

Shortly after the ferry left land, Eugene and I were leaning over the side, looking into the water.

"Johnny?" said Eugene in a quiet voice.

"Yes?"

"I have something to tell you, Johnny."

"Is it about the button?"

"Yes," he said, lowering his head. He paused a few moments before asking, "How did you know?"

"I kind of suspected something was up on the morning of the band concert. Even though you probably weren't really that excited about seeing the band, you seemed awfully happy, and I was trying to figure out why. Then, that night when I realized the button was missing, I put two and two together."

"You're right about that. I don't have music in my blood—well, at least I didn't until Mr. Puffer put it there." Eugene smiled.

I laughed. "It was your reaction to Miss O'Neill's scary story that confirmed it for me."

"That scared the daylights out of me, Johnny."

"Me too, actually," I admitted.

"Johnny, I'm sorry I took the button. That was wrong of me."

"Eugene, thanks for telling me. And Eugene, I forgive you."

I could tell that a lump welled up in Eugene's throat. He couldn't talk, but he had a smile on his face.

A few minutes later, I said, "Eugene, I have something

to confess to you too."

He looked at me with a quizzical expression. "What is it?"

"I wasn't really counting steps from Polk City to Nebraska. I just wanted to distract you so that you'd stop pestering me about seeing the button."

"Well, I kind of figured that out, at least the part about not really counting the steps."

"How'd you figure that out?"

"Easy. On the last day, I counted your steps instead of mine. The number you told me wasn't anywhere close to the actual number you walked."

"Wow, you counted all my steps?"

"I sure did," he said. "That was pretty intense!"

We both laughed.

"I'm glad we're friends now, Eugene."

"Me too, Johnny."

As we approached the opposite shore, Eugene and I joined the rest of our group.

"Eugene, you look awfully happy today," said Kate, grinning herself.

"I learned a lesson, waiting for our turn on the ferry."

"What lesson was that, Eugene?" I asked.

"Well, the whole time we were waiting to cross, everybody around us was whining and complaining, just as I used to do, and they were quite unhappy. But Mr. Stevens set the example for us—he didn't complain, so neither did we. And you know what? Though we didn't get on the ferry any sooner than we would have if we had complained, we were happy. The old Eugene Dinwidden III would have complained. I prefer your approach, Mr.

Stevens. I'm not going to complain ever again."

Pa smiled. "Well, you know, Eugene, ever is a long time, but it seems to me that you're on the right track. The attitude of not complaining is supposed to be the normal attitude—I don't think God is too keen with our whining."

When we reached the opposite shore, Kate reached into the snow and pulled up a handful of dirt. "Johnny, this looks like Iowa dirt, it feels like Iowa dirt, and it even smells like Iowa dirt."

"Does it taste like Iowa dirt?" I asked.

"I'll let you be the judge of that," she laughed.

17
Nebraska City

There's a crossroads about two miles west from here, and then we'll head south to Auburn. From there, it's a straight shot west through Tecumseh and on to Red Cloud," said Pa the next morning, as we began our journey westward from Nebraska City.

I was tired and my eyes were feeling droopy. The rhythm of Millie and Billy's steps, combined with the sound of the wagons' wheels rolling along a dirt road, made a kind of clip-a-clop, clip-a-clop, thump thump, clip-a-clop, clip-a-clop, thump thump sound that was lulling me to sleep. I don't know if it's possible to fall asleep while walking, but if it is, I did.

Even in my sleep, from somewhere in the back of my mind I heard a new pattern, a clippety-clop, clippety-clop that was moving along at a quick, steady beat.

"Whoa!" said Pa. Millie and Billy obeyed immediately.

Pa's voice snapped me awake. I opened my eyes only to see a man on a horse approach us from behind, overtaking our wagons.

"Pa," whispered Kate, "who is he?"

"Don't know," said Pa.

"Hello, folks," said the man, wearing a black jacket and

a white hat. He had a red handkerchief around his neck.

"Morning," said Pa.

"Heading to Lancaster?" the man asked. He sat on a beautiful chestnut mare that had a white spot shaped like a big church bell under its neck.

I glanced back and saw that Ott, Elias, and George had pulled out their rifles and were eyeing the man warily.

"Lancaster? Maybe," replied Pa. He didn't want to share our plans with a stranger.

"Did I say Lancaster? I'm sorry, I meant Lincoln," the man chuckled. "Before Lincoln was Lincoln, Lincoln was Lancaster."

"He's confusing. He sounds like Ott," whispered Kate.

"Allow me to introduce myself," said the man. "My name is Appling, Victor Appling, but you can call me Vic. I'm a bounty hunter."

"Are you looking for anyone in particular?"

"Lookin' for a scoundrel who goes by the name of Buck Sewell."

"Haven't seen or met anyone by that name," said Pa.

"You'd know him if you saw him. He's got a big old scar across his chin, and his nose is kinda bent to one side. And he's meaner than a rattler that's been stepped on. I am convinced that he's in the area, maybe the immediate area."

Pa didn't respond. He seemed to be thinking about something. Mr. Appling remained silent for a moment but then continued. "Listen, I am heading to Lincoln. I don't want to intrude in your business, but if you're going that way too, perhaps we can join forces. At least, I can be on the lookout and help protect y'all at the same time."

"Mr. Appling, we appreciate your offer, but I cannot

afford the cost that your protection would require. I—"

"Please, call me Vic. Mister ... uh ... I'm sorry, I didn't catch your name."

"I didn't give my name," said Pa.

"Oh, right. Well, sir, I'm not asking for money. I'm just offering to ride along with you all on my way back to Lincoln, if it's okay with you. Where are y'all from?"

"You'd get to Lincoln quicker if you went on ahead. We aren't moving all that fast," said Pa, not answering his question.

"Well, that's true," said Mr. Appling, "but I see it like this. If Sewell does show himself, then I can help defend you. And I'm confident that I could then bring him into custody."

"So ... what you're saying is that we're kind of like bait, hoping to draw Sewell out from hiding," said Pa.

"Well, you're bait anyway," said Mr. Appling, "whether I'm here with you or not."

Pa pondered this a bit and nodded. "I guess you've got a good point there, Mr. Appling."

"So let's try this again," said Mr. Appling. "Where are y'all from?"

"Polk City," answered Pa.

"Polk City? Why, do you know Rafe Ledbetter? He's my brother-in-law."

Mr. Ledbetter ran the general store in Polk City. We liked him. That was good enough for Pa.

"Boys, put down your guns," said Pa. "My name is Stevens, John Stevens, and we are on our way to Red Cloud and possibly beyond. I wasn't planning on going through Lincoln. I was going to turn south here, go down to Auburn, and then steer toward Tecumseh."

"It's a pleasure to meet you, Mr. Stevens. Now, about your itinerary, I wouldn't go down to Auburn if I were you," said Mr. Appling. "First off, that's where Sewell was last seen. Second, the Indians in Kansas, just south of Auburn and Tecumseh, have been unhappy recently and there's talk of an uprising, maybe some attacks."

"So you would suggest going through Lincoln?"

"Yes, I would. I would head west to Syracuse and then cut northwest to Lincoln."

"And heading south when?"

"I'd probably go through Lincoln, then through Milford, and then drop down through Friend, Hastings, and

Red Cloud."

"What'll it cost us, time-wise?" asked Pa.

"Oh, it'll take a couple extra days to head up to Lincoln, but the Nebraska City-Fort Kearny Trail is a good road and it's much safer than the back roads."

Pa looked at Ma. I never could tell what Ma was thinking, but somehow Pa could.

"Well … you've talked me into it. The Nebraska City-Fort Kearny Trail it is. Mr. Appling—Vic—I invite you to ride along with us," said Pa, and Ma smiled.

"Mr. Stevens, I'm much obliged."

"Just call me John. I apologize for my rudeness," said Pa. "I guess I'm a bit jumpy from an earlier encounter we had with two men on horseback who tried to rob us."

"Where was this?"

"Just outside of Shenandoah, Iowa. We were saved by some expert marksmanship, the arrival of a posse, and the deft use of a cane," Pa said with a smile.

"Well sir," said Mr. Appling, "my goal is to eliminate highway crime in this area, and I think I can best do that by tracking down fugitives like Sewell."

The rest of the day, as we worked our way to Syracuse, Mr. Appling told us story upon story about life in Nebraska and points west.

"So, as I was sayin' earlier," said Mr. Appling, "Lincoln started off as Lancaster, a small village not much bigger than your thumbnail, south of the Platte River.

"Now, many Nebraskans who lived south of the Platte were southern sympathizers during the war, and there was concern that Kansas, the next state south, would try to annex southern Nebraska.

"The rest of the people in the state, of course, didn't

want to divide Nebraska, so a bunch of folks proposed movin' the state capital from Omaha to Lancaster, hopin' that having the capital there would make the southern folks feel more like Nebraskans.

"Well, the folks from Omaha got all uppity about movin' the capital—they didn't want to give that up—so they got the state government to change the name of the town from Lancaster to Lincoln. They knew the southern folks wouldn't like a town with the name of the northern president, and the politicians in Omaha figured that was the way to keep the capital in Omaha."

"It obviously didn't work," I said, jumping into the conversation without really intending to.

Mr. Appling smiled. "No sir, it didn't. Lincoln became the capital of Nebraska anyway, in about 1876—just two years ago. The government moved out of Omaha, and now Lincoln is blossomin' like a big red rose in my granny's garden."

"How long have you lived in Nebraska?" asked Eugene.

"I reckon I've been here just over five years," said Mr. Appling. "I hail from western Illinois originally, but I now call Nebraska home."

We reached Syracuse by nightfall. Looking west across Nebraska, we watched the sun set.

That night, I was almost asleep when Kate whispered, "Johnny?"

"Yes, Kate?"

"You know how we watch the sun come up in the morning and go down at night?"

"Yes, what about it?"

"Well, you know how it's not really the sun going around the earth but the earth going around the sun, and the earth spins to give us day and night?"

"Yes, that's right."

"Well, how come it feels like we're the ones staying still, and the rest of the universe—the sun and stars and planets—seem to be the ones moving?"

"Good question. Maybe it's God's way of reassuring us."

"What do you mean?"

"Even though we might not be at the center of the universe, maybe God wants to remind us that he loves us like we are at the center."

"That's a good thought, Johnny."

"Good night, Kate."

"Good night, Johnny."

18
Syracuse

P a, are we going to make it to Lincoln today?" asked Kate the next morning as we were eating breakfast.
"No, sweetheart, we won't get there until tomorrow, Lord willing," said Pa.

As I sat there eating, I was thinking about the adventures we had experienced on our travels thus far, and I thought out-loud, "I wonder what adventure we'll see today?"

Ma laughed. "Well, Johnny, to be truthfully blunt, I hope and pray that we have no adventures today. How would you feel about a plain, ordinary day with no excitement and nothing, say, out of the ordinary to talk about years later."

"Well, a day without adventure certainly would be unique, at least for this trip, so I guess I could go along with that," I said, smiling.

Those of us who were hoping for a plain, ordinary day would soon be disappointed.

After breakfast, Pa and George worked on hitching up the horses while the rest of us were loading the wagons. George was helping for the first time since the wolf attack, moving slowly and stiffly. It was good to see him

126

up on his feet, though it did throw off our routine, affecting the timing of when things were done.

Pa and George finished hitching up the third wagon, and Pa handed the reins to Ott. Moments later, Elias said, "Ott, I'm going to lift up the little stove."

Ott dropped the reins, stood up, and stepped from the seat into the wagon box. Elias lifted the little stove, and Ott grabbed hold of it.

Something—I don't know what it was, whether it was a noise or an animal hiding in the woods or just a bad dream—spooked one or both of the horses, and like a thunderbolt they instantly took off in a full speed gallop! The stove was ripped out of Elias's and Ott's hands and fell to the ground with a crash. Ott somehow was still on the wagon, thrown to his knees. The reins were dragging on the ground beneath the wagon and there was no way Ott would be able to reach them.

The horse-drawn wagon raced down the road, totally out of control. Somehow the wagon missed colliding with our other wagons, and then the horses veered left into a field. The wagon began bouncing and bucking like a wild stallion in a rodeo. Ma screamed.

By this time, Elias had leaped onto Blackie, the spare horse, and Mr. Appling had quickly mounted his horse, and they sped across the field to rescue Ott and corral the wagon.

Once or twice the wagon went up on two wheels and almost toppled sideways, but somehow it righted itself. The horses seemed to be going faster and faster. The wagon hit a mound and Ott was tossed up in the air, landing on the ground behind the wagon!

Mr. Appling motioned to Elias, pointing to Ott. Elias

stopped and dismounted when he reached Ott, while Mr. Appling continued gaining ground on the wagon. He brought his horse alongside the two galloping horses, reached over and grabbed the reins of the horse nearest to him, and was able to slow them down, bringing them to a stop.

Elias yelled something, but we couldn't hear him. Then he gave us a signal that everything was okay. He helped Ott up off the ground. Ott waved back to us. He was fine.

Ott and Elias brought the horses and wagon back. We were fortunate that Mr. Appling had been able to get the runaway horses to stop. There seemed to be no damage to them, and the wagon—even the wagon wheels—suffered no harm.

"That was some nice ridin'," said Pa. "Mighty nice."

"Thank you. I've seen a few runaway wagons in my day," replied Mr. Appling.

The real miracle was how Ott escaped unscathed. He was muddy but had been spared injury. What could have been tragic ended up being merely terrifying.

Ma gave Ott a hug and said, "I thought we agreed that today was to be a calm, rather uneventful day."

"I know, I know," said Ott. "Maybe we can save that for tomorrow."

"Mr. Appling?" asked Kate, as we walked along on our way toward Lincoln.

"Yes, my dear?" Mr. Appling had a smile on his face.

"Have you ever met a real Indian?"

A scowl quickly crossed his face like a thundercloud coming out of nowhere.

"If I never see another Injun in my life, it'll be too soon," said Mr. Appling.

"So, you have seen an Indian?" asked Kate.

"Yes, I have. I've seen more than my share."

"Are you afraid of Indians?"

Mr. Appling coughed, and then he cleared his throat, but he didn't say anything. I think Kate realized she had stumbled onto a topic that Mr. Appling apparently didn't want to talk about, so she prudently remained silent.

After a few minutes, Mr. Appling cleared his throat again and said, "Afraid of Injuns? No, I'm not. I'm afraid of how I might respond if I were to see an Injun, though."

"What do you mean?" I asked.

"A man can get arrested for killing someone these days," said Mr. Appling. "At least, that's what they tell me. I'm afraid that if I were somehow alone in a room with an Injun, only one man would walk out of that room, and it wouldn't be the Injun."

A look of shock appeared on Kate's face. "But Mr. Appling, God wants us to love our neighbors."

"Being a neighbor works both ways," said Mr. Appling.

"What do you mean?" asked Kate.

"If they are my neighbor, then I am their neighbor. If they want me to … to treat them as a neighbor deserves, they need to treat me as I deserve. It's as simple as that."

"Well, but Mr. Appling, I don't think God said that we are to love our neighbors only if they love us too."

"Yes, that's probably true," he said, "but it's hard to love a neighbor when he has brought me so much pain."

"Why is that, Mr. Appling?" asked Kate.

"Kate, dear, that's enough. Sometimes adults don't want to say everything they're thinking," said Pa. "Children shouldn't pry."

Mr. Appling was silent and seemed to be in deep thought.

Meanwhile, the wagon wheels continued rolling.

Later that afternoon, when we stopped for the day—about halfway between Syracuse and Lincoln—a light snow began to fall from the darkening sky.

"Johnny, Eugene," said Pa, handing me a .22 rifle, "go out and see if you can find a bit of meat to add to our supper."

"But … but Mr. Stevens," stammered Eugene, "I'm no good at shooting a gun, and I've never hunted."

"I understand that, Eugene, but it's like anything else worth doing. Learning to handle a gun takes time and practice, and you gotta start somewhere. Johnny can show you how it's done—just be sure to do what he says."

"Yes sir," said Eugene. Pa patted him on the shoulder, and off we went.

As we walked toward a wooded area on the other side of the road, Eugene said, "I'm kind of surprised that your father trusts me with a gun. After all, I have only fired one shot in my life, and that was the shot that blew Mother's dress to smithereens."

"Well, Eugene," I said, "Pa has seen a change in you."

"I hope I can make up for—"

"Shh!" I said, holding my hand up to hush Eugene. "There is a rabbit nearby," I whispered, pointing to fresh tracks in the snow. It wasn't long before we found the rabbit that was attached to those tracks.

"There he is, all plump and ready for supper," I whispered. "You wanna take the first shot?"

"No, you go right ahead. I'm still learning all of this."

"Okay. Now, the rifle is already loaded, but if it weren't,

here's where you put the bullet in." I went through the motions of inserting a bullet.

"Johnny?"

"Just a second, Eugene. Now, when you take aim at something, you have to think about what's beyond the target, because that bullet can fly a long ways."

"Johnny?"

"I usually try to shoot kind of downwards, so that if I miss, the bullet just goes into the ground."

"Johnny?"

"What is it, Eugene?"

"Where's the rabbit?"

I looked where the rabbit had been, and he was gone.

"Well … I think we just saw a live demonstration of the first rule of shooting a rabbit," I said.

"What's that?" asked Eugene.

"You need a rabbit to shoot at."

Eugene laughed.

We continued our search for rabbits, and it wasn't long before we found another one, almost as big as the first one we had seen.

I got the rabbit on the first shot and we put him in a knapsack. Soon after that, another adult rabbit came scampering by, and I got that one too. Two rabbits in the bag meant that we were off to a good start.

A bit later, we saw a squirrel foraging in the snow, and I told Eugene to give it a try. He said he was afraid he might miss, and I told him it was okay if he missed the squirrel, that he had to try eventually anyway.

He aimed carefully—his gun was very steady—and pulled the trigger. The snow flew up just in front of the squirrel, and the squirrel scampered off.

"Missed him," Eugene said. "Sorry."

"Hey Eugene, no need to apologize. You're learning how to shoot that thing. Besides, we all miss now and then. Even Pa misses sometimes."

"Really?"

"Really."

Eugene had three more missed shots before he got one, a nice, plump squirrel, and we put it in the bag. Eugene was beaming.

When we had three rabbits and four squirrels in the bag, we decided that was probably enough for the time being, and we headed back to the camp. What we found when we reached the wagons was Miss O'Neill sitting around a campfire with the others. She was telling them some kind of story.

… and then Nobbin said to Hobbin, "See that dog on the other side of the field? Let's race to the dog and I'll prove that I'm a faster horse than you are." Hobbin agreed. Nobbin said, "One, two, three, go!"

So they were off. Nobbin had the lead at first, but then Hobbin caught up. Then Hobbin led for a while, but soon Nobbin caught up. And then the lead went back and forth: Hobbin, then Nobbin, then Hobbin, then Nobbin, then Nobbin, then Nobbin, then Hobbin, and then Hobbin Nobbin Nobbin Hobbin Hobbin Hobbin Hobbin Hobbin Nobbin Hobbin Nobbin Nobbin Hobbin Hobbin Nobbin … the race was close, oh so close, and as they approached the dog it was Hobbin and then Nobbin and then

Nobbin and then Hobbin and … finally … they both passed the dog.

The dog shouted, "It's a tie!"

Hobbin turned to the other horse, Nobbin, and said, "Look, Nobbin, it's a talking dog!"

A long pause allowed the air to be filled with silence, and then Miss O'Neill uttered those dreaded words, "The end."

Ma and Pa groaned; Mr. Appling, Ott and Mr. Dinwidden chuckled; and Elias, George, and Mrs. Dinwidden looked perplexed.

"The end?" said Mrs. Dinwidden.

"Is that really the end?" asked George.

"Wait, the story can't end like that," said Elias.

"Sorry folks, that's how the story ends," said Miss O'Neill with a smile. "Besides, I think it's time for me to start working on supper."

"Me too," said George. "What did our mighty hunters bring home?"

"Show 'em, Eugene," I said.

Eugene proudly held up the bag and announced, "We have four squirrels and three rabbits!" He was wearing the biggest smile I had seen him wear yet.

The next thing to do was clean the animals. I got out my knife and showed Eugene how to do it. I cleaned one rabbit and one squirrel, and I even showed him how to find and remove the scent glands in the squirrel's armpits— I never noticed a difference in how the glands affected the taste of the squirrel, but Ma said it gave the meat a "gamey" taste, and she wouldn't eat it if the scent glands hadn't been removed—and then I handed the knife to

Eugene. He tried as best as he could, but he pretty much mangled the squirrel. It would still be edible, but it wasn't exactly something that could be identified as a particular animal. He just needed more practice. He was a quick learner, and the next squirrel that Eugene cleaned turned out almost perfect. He cleaned the rest of the game, too.

Eugene was almost giddy with excitement. "Johnny, thanks for showing me how to hunt and skin the animals." I smiled and nodded. This was a different Eugene, for sure.

While four squirrels and three rabbits didn't hardly add up to be a feast—after all, there were twelve of us, counting Mr. Appling—it was enough to keep us content and satisfied.

That night as I lay in bed trying to fall asleep, my mind kept repeating the words Mr. Appling had said: *It's hard to love a neighbor when he has brought me so much pain.*

What pain had the Indians given him? Why did he hate them?

I tossed and turned for quite a while before falling asleep. I would have slept better if I had known that the answers to these questions—and the beginnings of new adventures—were just around the corner, on the other side of midnight.

19
Lincoln

Lincoln was still a few miles away when we started off the next morning, our second day out of Syracuse. The sunny, blue sky, accompanied by a warm westerly wind rushing across the plains, should have lifted my spirits and gotten my day off to a cheerful start. It did neither of those.

"Why the long face, Johnny?" asked George.

"I dunno," I said.

"Yes, you do."

"No … well, yeah, maybe I do," I said softly.

Mr. Appling was riding his horse alongside the lead wagon. I was walking with the third wagon at the back of the pack.

"Does it have something to do with Mr. Appling and the Indians?" asked George.

"Yes, it does," I admitted. "I like Mr. Appling and all. It's just that … it's just that it bothers me that he seems to dislike all Indians because some Indian hurt him. That's not right. That's not how it should be."

"I agree with you, Johnny. I think you're probably right. Before you start feeling too high and mighty, though, may I offer you a couple of things to keep in mind?"

"Yeah, I guess so."

"First of all, we have no idea what Mr. Appling experienced. We don't know what happened to cause his dislike of Indians—justified or not—and we also don't really know how we would respond in the same situation."

"Okay, I understand that," I said.

"Second," continued George, "maybe he just hasn't met enough Indians, or perhaps he's only met the bad eggs and not the good ones."

"Maybe, I don't know. George, do you think it is possible for a grown-up to change his heart?"

"Johnny, have you ever heard of Chester Hutcheson?"

"Kind of. He was a potter in Polk City once upon a time, right?"

"Yep. Well, he was the best potter for miles around. The beauty of his work, unsurpassed in quality and attention to detail, was respected by everyone. He was also a generally likable fellow, except for one significant problem."

"What was that?"

"He didn't like Negroes."

"He didn't like any of them?"

"Nope."

"Why not?"

"That was just how he had set his mind. He had never actually met a Negro, but he had heard stories, lies, and myths, and he just decided that Negroes were no good. People tried talking sense into him, but he would have none of it. He became bitter and angry anytime the subject was mentioned."

"So what happened?"

"Well, Chester's eyesight began failing. He could still make out shapes and shadows, but he couldn't see detail.

A potter needs to be able to see his intricate designs, so he decided to hire someone to apprentice under him. He hired Robert Powell."

"Robert Powell? But he's—"

"Yep. Now keep quiet and I'll tell you the rest of a story that Pa told me a few years ago." George began:

> So, the story goes that old Chester hired Robert Powell, but he didn't realize that Robert wasn't white. Nobody else was going to tell Chester, for fear of incurring his wrath. All Chester could discern was that Robert was dependable, hard-working, and honest, and he was a gifted, quick learner. In almost no time, Robert became an outstanding potter in his own right and made Chester's business more successful than it had ever been.
>
> Then one day Chester said something mean about Negroes, and Robert said, "Mr. Hutcheson, why don't you like black folks?"
>
> Chester replied, "I've never met one who was good for anything."
>
> Robert looked at him and said, "Well, why did you hire one then?"
>
> "Why did ..." began Chester, echoing Robert's words. Then you know what he did? He began chuckling, then laughing harder, and finally he was rolling on the floor in hysterics.
>
> "Ha! Robert Powell! Why, you're a Negro! I never knew!" exclaimed Mr. Hutcheson, who then fell on his knees and said, "Mr. Powell, please, please forgive me. I've been so wrong my

whole life. If I could have seen who you are, I must admit I wouldn't have taken you on as an apprentice. But you have opened my eyes. Oh, my, I've been so wrong, so, so wrong." Chester began weeping.

"Mr. Hutcheson," said Robert, "you don't need my forgiveness. You have always treated me for who I am—the work I do, the values I have, what I stand for—and not by the color of my skin."

"Mr. Powell, you are my equal," said Chester. "In fact, Robert, you are a better man than I."

Chester's life was changed. He became a happy fellow who enjoyed the company of those all around him. When he died a year or two later, he left his entire pottery business to Robert.

"So, Johnny," continued George, "you never really know how someone's going to end up."

"Thanks, George. I needed to hear that story."

"Don't give up on him, Johnny. There is always hope."

George was right. There was always hope. With a sudden burst of energy, I raced ahead and caught up with the lead wagon, joining in step with Kate and Eugene. There I found Mr. Appling and Ma talking.

"You are fond of Lincoln, Mr. Appling. Have you ever lived there?" asked Ma.

"Well, yes and no. To be precise, I have a place of residence in Lincoln—a room I rent from a spinster on the north side—but I'm hardly ever there. Yep, I moved to Lincoln right after ... after my brother Floyd was killed."

"Oh, I'm sorry," said Ma.

"Thank you, Mrs. Stevens. Floyd's death is something I've had to work hard to come to terms with, something that gave my faith a terrible shake. I still sometimes struggle with it, especially when I'm caught off-guard, as happened yesterday when I was asked about Injuns."

Mr. Appling was silent for a few moments, as if deliberating something, and then he told his story:

There are days when I think that I have gotten over it, that it's all behind me. Then there are days like yesterday when I'm reminded of the horrible events.

The Black Hawk War back in '32 was where it all started. You young'uns might not know the story behind this, so allow me to tell you. Black Hawk was a chief who led an army of Injuns into western Illinois to reclaim land that he believed the U.S. government had cheated from the Injuns.

There was a bad feelin' between Injuns and the settlers, and battles sprang up all over the place.

My grandparents—my mother's parents— lived in a settlement on Injun Creek in western Illinois. Mother was fifteen years old.

One of the settlers dammed up the creek so that he could irrigate his fields, which angered the Injuns livin' downstream because they depended on Injun Creek for fish and water. The Injuns tried to reason with the settler, but he would have none of it. They warned him that they were serious, but he simply ignored them.

The infuriated Injuns attacked the Injun Creek settlement, killin' several men, women, and children, and kidnappin' two of the girls. My grandfather was one of the men killed. They ... they scalped him.

One of the kidnapped girls was my mother.

The Injuns held her captive for two weeks and then let her go. Even years later, when Mother was busy raisin' a family of three boys, she never talked much about the incident, but she was always havin' nightmares and tellin' us how afraid she was of Injuns.

Now Floyd, my youngest brother, grew up with a natural bent toward history, military, and politics. Of the three brothers—Floyd, our older brother Wright, and me—Floyd was by far the most warrior-like. He was afraid of nothin', and it wasn't uncommon to see him pick a fight with someone twice his size if he thought justice needed to be served. He was always itchin' to prove he was tougher than the next guy. He was always wantin' a battle. He was always wantin' a war.

When the War Between the States broke out in '61, Wright and I signed up with the 4th Illinois Infantry. Floyd was twelve, too young to join the Union army. He was angry that he couldn't be part of the confrontation. He wanted to experience the heat of battle: the blazing, thundering cannons; the bullets whizzing by, overhead; and the aromas of smoke, sweat, gunpowder, and blood, all mixed together in a fragrance that smelled like war.

Mother told Floyd that he could show his courage by working hard at home on the farm. After all, Father had passed away several years earlier and Mother needed Floyd's help on the farm. Floyd understood his role, and he devoted himself to it. He became an excellent farmer.

Still, every two or three days, Floyd would go to the general store and see if there was any news of the war, any soldiers coming home on leave, or if there were updated casualty lists. Floyd heard and read about stories of bravery and courage, stories of gallantry and honor, stories of hope and worthy causes.

Then, one day Mother and Floyd received a letter that read, "Dearest Mother and Floyd, It is with great regret and grief that I must tell you this news. Wright fell at Vicksburg, Miss. He died valiantly. He died serving his country." The letter was from me.

The news of Wright's death propelled Floyd back into an intense interest in war. Mother recognized this, and she asked Floyd to promise that he would continue running the farm, at least until he was eighteen. Floyd agreed to that, but in his heart he was ready to join the military.

Floyd kept his promise. In fact, he stayed on the farm until he was twenty-five. Mother died in 1873. She left the farm to Floyd and me in her will, but I didn't want to return to the farm, and Floyd was anxious to leave. So, within six months after Mother died, we sold the farm, and

Floyd joined the U.S. Army, Seventh Cavalry. That was in 1874.

Floyd wrote me a letter the night before he was dispatched. "I'm free! I'm free to prove my courage. I'm free to do my part to ensure that tomorrow morning you will still find Old Glory waving sharply in the breeze."

Floyd was dispatched to Fort Abraham Lincoln in the Dakota Territory as part of an expedition to explore the Black Hills region for natural resources, including gold. Now, a substantial portion of the territory had been promised to the Sioux by the US government. Gold, indeed, was found—not very much, but enough—and settlers began streaming into the territory. The Injuns were not happy about that.

Tensions flared in the Sioux tribes, and finally, in the summer of '76, there was a fight at Little Big Horn in Montana. A band of Injuns, mostly Sioux, met the Seventh Cavalry head on. The Seventh was led by George Custer. You probably know the rest of the story. We never heard from Floyd again.

Floyd was the only family that I had left. And now he was gone.

A lump formed in my throat.

"And now you know," said Mr. Appling, "why I don't like Injuns. I understand why they resented giving up their territory—the U.S. government treated them terribly—and, if I were in their shoes, I'd be angry too. But I can't love them. It's just too hard."

Everyone was quiet after that, and we walked pretty much the rest of the way to Lincoln in silence.

We arrived in Lincoln just before noon, and Mr. Appling led us straight-away to what he claimed was the best restaurant in town.

"Victor, my friend, velcome," shouted a man who opened the door as we approached the restaurant. "And who are zese people you brought vit you? Hello, my name is Nikolai, and zis is my restaurant."

Mr. Nikolai wasn't from around there—you could tell that by his accent—but I had no idea where he was from. A family from England had moved to Polk City a couple of years back, so I was familiar with an English accent. Nikolai had nowhere close to an English accent. He used "z" sounds where he should have used "th" sounds, and I had no idea what language that was from.

"This is the Stevens family, the Dinwiddens, and Miss Lucille O'Neill," said Mr. Appling, "and I met them on the way here from Nebraska City." Mr. Appling's smile had returned.

"Velcome!" said Mr. Nikolai. "Any friend of Victor's is a friend of mine. Do please come in." He led us to a table as he was talking. "Vould you like some dinner? I made a very nice pork roast today, and zere is still plenty. Please, please be seated."

Ma looked at Pa. Pa nodded, and Ma nodded, and I guess that meant we were going to sit down and eat in Mr. Nikolai's restaurant.

"Nikki," said Mr. Appling, "I am expecting Bill here at any moment. Is it okay if we wait for him before ordering?"

"Yes, of course," said Mr. Nikolai.

Bill? Who was this Bill that Mr. Appling mentioned? I didn't know, but I knew that I would soon find out.

We all sat down and for the first few minutes I just looked around the room, watching people as they ate and chatted. There were all kinds of people there—some were dressed more formally than others, but everyone was dressed up to some extent, whether it be a banker, lawyer, or someone who had spent the morning working the "back forty."

The restaurant door opened, and the silhouette of a man stood there in the doorway as the din in the restaurant became a hushed silence.

"Who's that?" I whispered to Mr. Appling.

"That's Bill Cody," he whispered back.

20
Elephant Bill

The man at the door had an imposing and commanding presence, though he wasn't taller than six feet, if even that. It was the way he carried himself that made people sit up and take notice. One quick look at his face and I knew that this man had stories to tell.

Mr. Nikolai greeted him as he walked in. They said something to each other, and I saw Mr. Nikolai motioning back toward our table. The man walked toward us. Mr. Appling stood up.

"Victor, how have you been?" the man boomed. Everyone in the restaurant turned and looked at us.

"Actually quite good, Bill, all things considered," said Mr. Appling. "Bill Cody, I want you to meet some friends of mine—Mr. and Mrs. Stevens, Mr. and Mrs. Dinwidden, and Miss O'Neill. We rode together from Nebraska City." Mr. Cody sat down at our table, between Mr. Appling and Pa, across from Kate and me.

"Now, Bill," began Mr. Appling, "the telegram you sent me in Nebraska City said you had a proposition you wanted to discuss with me."

"Whoa there, just a moment," said Mr. Cody. "Food

145

before business, I always say. Besides, I'm thirsty!" He held up his hand, and a waiter immediately came to our table.

"I need a drink before we order our meals. I'll have the usual," said Mr. Cody.

"Yes sir," said the waiter, "coming right up."

"Johnny," whispered Kate, "what's a 'usual'?"

"I don't know, Kate."

Soon it was Kate's turn to order.

"And what would you like to drink, Miss?"

Kate hemmed and hawed a little and then said, "I'll have the usual, too."

"The usual?" asked the waiter, confused.

"Yes sir—the same thing he's having," she said, pointing to Mr. Cody.

"Um … uh … okay," said the waiter. "No problem."

The waiter brought Mr. Cody his drink, and for Kate he brought a large lemonade. It didn't seem to bother Kate that her drink was larger and a different color than Mr. Cody's.

Mr. Cody glanced across the table at Kate. "What's your name, Sugar?" he asked.

She looked at him shyly and answered, "My name is Kate."

"Glad to meet you, Kate. My name is Bill."

"Bill here is a hunter," said Mr. Appling, "a very good one. He's made quite a name for himself. Most folks out this way call him Buffalo Bill."

"So … you hunt buffaloes?" asked Kate.

"Well, I do now. I used to hunt elephants," said Mr. Cody with a straight face.

"Elephants? There were elephants out here?"

"Yep, elephants, back in the day. They used to call me Elephant Bill."

"Elephant Bill? Really?"

"Yep. But then there was a problem."

"What was that?"

"We ran out of elephants."

"How did we run out of elephants?" asked Kate.

"I shot them all," said Mr. Cody. "Let me show you. Nikki, come here a moment, please," shouted Mr. Cody.

Mr. Nikolai walked over to our table.

"Nikki, can I order a bowl of elephant soup?" Mr. Cody asked with a wink.

"I'm sorry, Mr. Cody, but vee don't haff any elephant soup today."

"How about an elephant omelet?"

"No, sir. Sorry. Vee can't do zat eizer."

"Roast elephant?"

"No."

"Elephant steak?"

"No."

"Elephant sauteed in butter?"

"No."

"Can I order anything with elephant in it?"

"Vell, not really."

"Why is that?"

"Vee haff run out of elephant, sir."

"Are you expecting to have elephant any time soon?"

"No sir. In fact, sir, I believe zat you haff shot all zee elephants zat ver around here."

"Ah, that explains it," said Mr. Cody. "Now, let me ask you this. Is it possible to get a bowl of buffalo soup?"

"Yes sir. Vee haff plenty of buffalo available. I can serve you buffalo escalloped, buffalo ground, buffalo roasted, buffalo au gratin, and, of course, buffalo steaks."

"I'm happy to hear that. Where did you get the buffalo?"

"From you, sir."

"Thanks, Nikki. So you see," said Mr. Cody, turning back toward Kate, "I have had to switch from hunting elephants to hunting buffaloes. That's why they call me Buffalo Bill."

"I understand," said Kate, "but I'm sorry you had to change your name from Elephant Bill to Buffalo Bill. I kind of like the sound of Elephant Bill."

Mr. Cody looked at Kate for a moment, not sure whether she was serious. I wasn't sure either.

"Well, Sugar, you can call me Elephant Bill."

"Thank you, Mr. Cody—I mean Elephant Bill."

The food was wonderful—vonderful, as Mr. Nikolai would say—and I ate more than I had perhaps ever eaten in one sitting. So stuffed that I could barely move, I sat in my chair and listened to Mr. Cody and Mr. Appling talk business.

"Victor, let me get to the point," said Mr. Cody. "You are well aware that I've put together an entertaining play that

I call *Scouts of the Plains*."

"Of course. I was at your show in St. Louis last year, remember?"

"Right. Now, the proposition I have for you is two-pronged."

"Let me guess," said Mr. Appling. "You want me to join your show."

"Well, yes and no," said Mr. Cody. "I want you to become part of our troupe so that you can learn the business. See, I'm hoping to get another project underway that involves creating a whole "Wild West" show, not just a play."

"Why do you want me?" asked Mr. Appling.

"You've got a much keener mind for business and numbers than I do."

"When does the new show start?"

"Oh, I don't know yet. It's a ways out there, maybe three, four years at the soonest. A wagon-load of planning has to be done first."

"So I'd be able to come in at the very beginning and help put this thing together?"

"Exactly."

"I need to think about this, Bill," said Mr. Appling.

"Of course you do. But don't think too hard. I don't know how long I can keep this opportunity open. I know that others are interested. You're my first choice, though."

"Thanks, Bill," said Mr. Appling.

They talked for another half-hour or so, chatting about the war, about Injuns, about hunting buffalo, about everything, it seemed.

I tried to be polite and pay attention, but my eyes were tired and I drifted off to sleep.

Marked with war paint, Black Hawk and several of his meanest, toughest warriors crashed through the front door of the house. I knew what they wanted—me!

Kate happened to be with me.

"Zere zey are!" snarled Black Hawk, in some kind of European accent.

"Vat about zee girl?" asked one of the warriors.

"Capture her too," commanded the chief.

"Come on, Kate!" I shouted. "Upstairs!"

Kate and I ran up the back staircase to the second floor, and then we scampered up the ladder to the attic. I locked the attic door, hoping it would buy us some time. The Indians quickly pursued us and soon were trying to knock down the door.

"The roof!" I yelled.

With an axe that I was fortunate to find on the floor at that moment, I broke through the wood shingles and we climbed out onto the roof.

I smelled smoke rising up from somewhere down below.

"They're burning the house!" Kate cried in dismay. "Oh, Johnny, what are we going to do?"

"Thunder! We need Thunder!" I said. I shouted, "Thunder, rescue us!" Within moments, I heard the hooves of my faithful friend.

"Okay, Kate, jump on three. One … two … THREE!"

Kate and I jumped off the roof, and with perfect timing, Thunder ran around the corner of the house, and Kate and I landed on his back. He happened to be saddled, which worked out conveniently.

I turned Thunder around and headed for the front door of the house.

"Johnny, where are we going? We should get out of here."

"Kate, as long as Black Hawk has free reign, nobody is safe. We must capture him!"

"Tell you what, Johnny," said Mr. Appling, snapping me awake, "this man could teach you a thing or two about huntin'. He's the epitome of the famous buffalo hunter."

Mr. Cody laughed. "Famous? I don't know about that. You are too kind, Victor. I'll have to admit, though, that I sure do enjoy the hunt."

Mr. Cody stood up from his chair and picked up his hat.

"You're not leaving us already, Bill?" said Mr. Appling.

"Well, Victor, I've got to be moving on. I'm supposed to be in North Platte in a couple of days to meet with some army folks."

Mr. Appling stood up and said, "Well then, I'll walk you to the door."

Mr. Cody turned to us and said, "Nice meeting you folks. Safe travels and good luck with finding a place to homestead. Bye, Sugar," he said, winking at Kate.

"Good-bye, Elephant Bill," said Kate, smiling.

I noticed that he stopped and handed Mr. Nikolai some money on his way out the door.

We sat and talked for another hour, maybe a little more, and then Pa said, "We best be gettin' on our way, too. Victor, what are your—"

BANG!

I heard a gunshot coming from outside!

BANG! BANG!

Two more shots were fired!

Mr. Nikolai rushed to the door and opened it wide. The street bustled with commotion.

"Vat is happenink?" he yelled.

"The bank's been robbed!" shouted a passerby.

"They're getting away!" said another.

"There were three of them, maybe four," said a third.

"Three, maybe four?" echoed Mr. Appling. "Could be the Buck Sewell gang!"

He stood up from his chair. "Nice meetin' all of you. Sorry to leave so abruptly." He nodded and was out the door almost before we knew it.

The street crowd disappeared eventually, and Pa said, "Let's try this again. We best be gettin' on our way."

Pa signaled to Mr. Nikolai, who came to our table.

"Mr. Nikolai, I'd like to settle up for the meal. How much do I owe you?"

Mr. Nikolai said, "It's already been paid. Mr. Cody took care off it on his vay out."

"Well, that was mighty nice of him!" exclaimed Ma. "If you see him again, please tell him thank you for us."

"Yes ma'am," said Mr. Nikolai.

Eugene walked next to me that afternoon as we made our way through Lincoln to a campground on the west side of town.

"Johnny," he said in a serious voice, "I've been thinking. We've got to start going after bigger game."

"What do you mean, Eugene?"

"I'm afraid that people are going to start calling us … Rabbit Johnny and Squirrel Eugene."

He broke into a big smile, and I laughed.

21
Milford

The next morning we headed out of Lincoln, moving westward. Ma was eager to get to Red Cloud, and Pa was itching to find a place of our own to settle.

We passed through Milford and found a place just on the other side where Pa decided that we would camp for the night.

"Johnny," said Ma, "when we were going through Milford, I saw a bakery selling fresh loaves of bread for ten cents each. Here's thirty cents. Run back to that bakery—it's not more than a quarter-mile from here, on the right side of the road, across from the barbershop in the middle of downtown—and buy three loaves for us."

"Sure, Ma, I'll be happy to. Anything else you want me to get?"

"No, I think bread will be enough."

I ran all the way downtown, easily finding the bakery. I walked into the shop, still breathing hard.

"Yes, young master," said the shopkeeper, "how can I help you today?"

"I would like three loaves of your bread, please."

"Three loaves? That will be fifteen cents."

"Fifteen? I thought it would be thirty. Aren't they a dime each?"

"In the afternoons, I sell the morning bread at half price because it's not quite as fresh. So, it's fifteen cents."

There I stood, alone in a bakery saturated with the aromas of breads, pastries, cookies, cakes, and chocolate, holding fifteen cents in my hand.

"How much are your cookies?" I asked.

"Two cookies for a nickel."

"Could I have six cookies please?" I asked before I knew what I was saying. Had I thought about it further, I would have realized it probably wasn't a good idea. It might spoil my appetite for supper. It might also get me in trouble with Ma or Pa.

But, before I could vocalize my thoughts, the six cookies were thrust upon me. I couldn't disappoint the shopkeeper by refusing the cookies, not now, not after I had verbally agreed to purchase them.

I accepted them humbly, and I decided to go ahead and enjoy them. After all, Ma had given me thirty cents for three loaves of bread. She was expecting me to return with three loaves and no money left over, and that's exactly how I would return.

I stepped out of the bakery and walked around to the back of the store, where I could sit down and enjoy my cookies in privacy. She had given me three chocolate cookies and three with oatmeal and raisins. I ate all six in rapid succession, wolfing them down as though I hadn't eaten for weeks.

It had been a long time since I had eaten that many cookies so quickly, and suddenly I didn't feel all that well. My stomach kind of hurt and I felt queasy. I was afraid of what might happen if I stood up too quickly.

I heard laughter coming from across the alleyway that separated the back of the bakery from the backyard of the house behind it. I looked, and for a moment I saw a girl, maybe my age, flying through the air, and then she disappeared, hidden from view by a small shed. Then she appeared again, and then disappeared, and I realized she was riding a large swing.

Suddenly, I forgot about my stomach, and I walked over to see what was happening. I turned the corner where I had seen her swinging. I found two girls, one about my age sitting on a swing and one maybe two years younger, standing by the swing. The older one had been swinging, and now it appeared that the younger one was going to take a turn. Then they saw me.

"Halloo," they called out. "Who are you?"

"I'm Johnny Stevens," I said. "I'm from Polk City, Iowa. Who are you?"

"I'm Lydia," said the older one.

"And I'm Chloe," said the younger. "Do you want to swing with us?"

"Sure, I would like that very much!" I said.

Before I knew it, I had swung for quite a while, and then Chloe swung for a good length of time, followed by Lydia doing the same. I was pushing Lydia and Chloe on the swing with all my might, and the swing was going so high that the girls would squeal and shriek and laugh, and they would cry, "Do it again! Do it again!"

I had just begun my third turn on the swing when something familiar caught my eye. I looked up and, in the gap between the bakery and the building just to the right of it, I saw Pa. He was walking toward the bakery.

I jumped off the swing and said, "Nice meeting you girls. Thanks for letting me swing, but I've got to go." I grabbed the three loaves of bread and raced down the street, trying to stay out of Pa's view.

When I returned to the campsite, Ma was waiting for me. She was not pleased.

"Johnny, it's been over an hour! What kept you so long? I finally had to send Pa after you. I was worried about your safety. I thought that perhaps something bad might have happened to you."

"I'm sorry, Ma. I saw these girls—Lydia and Chloe—playing on their swing, and they asked me if I wanted a turn. I guess I just lost track of time."

Ma sighed and shook her head in exasperation.

Ma, Mrs. Dinwidden, and Miss O'Neill began working on supper. I am sure that what they were cooking smelled wonderful, but the aroma reminded me of all the cookies I had eaten earlier in the afternoon, and that feeling of nausea began overwhelming me.

"Johnny," said Miss O'Neill, "you don't look so good."

"Oh, I'm okay Miss O'Neill. I feel fine."

"Johnny," she whispered, "you look about as green as a frog at noon. How many cookies did you have?"

"Cookies? Why are you asking about cookies?" I was shocked that she had guessed.

"Cookies or cakes or something, maybe chocolate … don't forget that I was once an eleven-year-old like you, and more than once I found myself standing alone in a bakery with money in my hand. I know the temptations that today's young ones can face."

"Wow, Miss O'Neill, you're amazing. Yes, I had cookies. I had six of them."

"Six cookies," she exclaimed. "You're going to have a difficult time with your dinner tonight, Johnny."

"I know," I said. "I didn't think of that in time, unfortunately. I just hope that Ma and Pa don't notice."

"Oh, I think they'll notice," said Miss O'Neill. "It wasn't like they just fell off the turnip wagon yesterday."

An hour after I returned to the camp site, Pa still had not come back.

"Maybe I'll have to send you to look for Pa," sighed Ma. "Wonder where he is?"

A few minutes later, Pa walked into the campsite and announced, "Here I am. Sorry, I got delayed." He set his knapsack down next to the wagon.

"Seems to run in the family," said Ma. "Anyway, now that you have returned, we can eat. We're all nearly famished!"

Ma served each of us a bowl of chicken and potato stew, one of my favorites. Ma gave me an extra large helping. Unfortunately, I wasn't hungry and my stomach still felt ill. I sat down and toyed with the food a little, trying not to look obvious in my attempt not to eat.

"Psst!"

I turned and saw Miss O'Neill subtly holding her bowl near mine. No one was looking, so I scooped a large portion of my stew into her bowl, and then I resumed acting as though I were eating.

"Here Johnny, have some more," said Ma, taking my bowl and refilling it before I could issue a protest.

All I could say was, "Thanks, Ma."

Again, Miss O'Neill edged her bowl near mine, and I again gave her the lion's share of what Ma had given me.

I breathed a sigh of relief when Ma announced that it

was time to clean up. That meant that supper was finished and I had successfully made it through the meal. I had regretted my actions, but at least it appeared that I hadn't gotten caught.

"Oh, Catherine, these are for tomorrow," said Pa, handing Ma two loaves of bread after we had finished cleaning. We were standing at our wagon, putting everything in order for the evening so that we could go to sleep.

"Two more loaves?"

"Yes," said Pa. "The bakery lady told me that she discounts the bread in the afternoon at half-price because it's not as fresh."

Uh oh.

"Johnny, do you have some money to give to me?" asked Ma. I think she knew the answer to her question, though.

"Well, Ma … Pa … I … uh … I was feeling hungry, and when I learned that the fifteen cents wouldn't be needed for the bread, I saw these cookies, and …"

"And bought six of them, eating them one after the other as fast as you could," said Pa.

"How'd … how'd you know?" I asked, astonished.

"The lady in the bakery told me," said Pa.

"How did she know to tell you?" I asked.

"She didn't really know that's what she was doing. I had asked her for a cookie, and she said they were all out. She said it was the darnedest thing, too, because she had only two customers come in who had bought cookies during the afternoon—a girl, right after lunch, and a young man, who had also bought three loaves of bread about an hour before I got there."

Pa continued. "She told me that shortly after she sold the cookies to the young man, she happened to glance out the window and saw the young man devouring the cookies like a hungry bear diving into a beehive full of honey. She laughed and said she had never seen anyone eat so many cookies so quickly."

"Johnny!" said Ma, disapprovingly. "Where is your sense of responsibility regarding how we use our money?"

"I'm sorry, Ma. I'm sorry, Pa. I didn't mean to disappoint you. I just … I just wasn't thinking, I guess."

"Always tell the truth, son. Sometimes not saying anything so that you will remain protected is the same as not telling the truth. Get it?"

"Got it."

"Good."

22
Friend

Warm, strong, westerly winds galloped across the plains of south central Nebraska that night. I woke up in the middle of the night in a sweat and tossed off the blankets. I heard coyotes howling somewhere way in the distance—too far away to be of any concern—and I suspected that they were either lamenting the end of winter or welcoming the beginning of spring. I wasn't sure which.

Pa and I were the first two up that morning. We started a campfire and put on a pot of water for coffee.

"The skies are dark this morning, Johnny."

"They look strange Pa, not like normal clouds. And it's so warm right now."

Pa was silent, just staring into the morning sky.

"Pa, how far are we from Red Cloud?"

"Well, if all goes according to plan, we should be entering Red Cloud about three days from now, God willing."

"When was the last time you saw Aunt Rachel Anne and Uncle Frank?"

"It was a few years after the Great Rebellion," said Pa. "They stopped by to see us on their way out to Red Cloud. That was just a year or so after you were born."

"I don't remember them," I said.

"I wouldn't expect you to. Ott was a toddler, and George and Elias were just little tykes."

"Why did they decide to go out to Red Cloud?"

"Good question, Johnny. The Great Rebellion was hard on Frank—it was hard on us all, really—and I remember Frank saying that he couldn't go back to his old, pre-war life. He had tried to make it work, but there were too many memories, too many ghosts. So, he decided to make a fresh start in a new place, and they chose Red Cloud."

"Red Cloud must have been a pretty new town back then. Were Uncle Frank and Aunt Rachel Anne the first settlers there?"

"They weren't the first, but that area was pretty much the western edge of the frontier at the time."

"Where did the name 'Red Cloud' come from?"

"Red Cloud is an Indian, a powerful chief from the Oglala Lakota tribe. He has caused a lot of problems for the U.S. military, but I haven't heard much about him for a few years. I'm pretty sure he's still alive though."

"I hope we don't run into him anytime soon."

"Me too, Johnny. Me too."

By mid-morning, we were nearing the town of Friend, Nebraska. The wind was still rushing at us, bringing intermittent pockets of warm and cool air. The skies, with thick, black clouds hovering overhead, had become increasingly dark. A major storm was brewing, and we were in the middle of it!

"John, we've got to find shelter," said Ma.

"I know. I've been thinking … didn't Sheriff Cogswell

tell us that he had a brother who lived in Friend?"

"That's right! Yes, he did. I remember because it's such an unusual name for a town."

"That's what I thought, too. Let's stop in town and ask where he lives."

"Do we have time before the storm?"

"I expect we have maybe an hour, hour and a half, before the storm unleashes its fury. I don't know what kind of storm it is, but it doesn't look good."

We hurried into Friend and stopped at the general store in the center of town. Pa and I went inside while the others waited outside. I think Pa liked taking me along because I could help him remember things he might forget. He sometimes said I was like his second brain.

"Mornin'," said the shopkeeper. "What can I do for you gentlemen?"

"Mornin'," said Pa. "We're wondering if you could tell us where someone by the name of Cogswell lives?"

"Would that be first name or last name?" the shopkeeper asked.

"Well … uh …"

"Just kiddin' you. You're looking for Charlie Cogswell, who lives less than a mile west of here. Just follow Main Street out of town. When you see a big, long fence on the right side of the road, that's the Cogswell farm. Their house is maybe a hundred yards from the gate, behind a windbreak of black walnut trees."

"Thanks," said Pa. "Let's go, Johnny." Pa and I raced out the door.

Not more than thirty minutes later, we pulled the wagons to a stop in a tidy, well-kept farm yard. Pa ran up to the door and knocked. Almost instantly the door opened, and we saw the spittin' image of Sheriff Cogswell.

"Hello, Mr. Cogswell? My name is Stevens, John Stevens, and we're from Polk City—"

"Polk City, Iowa," said Mr. Cogswell. "My brother wrote me. We can talk later. I assume you want to get in out of this weather."

"Well, yes sir, that would—"

"We need to get your horses under shelter. Put 'em in my barn. It's plenty big enough."

Mr. Cogswell stepped outside and quickly walked to the barn, opening the door. We unhitched the horses and led them into the barn just as the first big drops of rain began to fall.

"Whew, that was close," said Ott. "For a minute there, I thought that—"

"Everybody, listen to me," shouted Mr. Cogswell, with a sense of urgency in his voice. "I need you to do exactly as I say. Follow me to the root cellar. We have to take cover right away!"

"The root cellar?" asked Mrs. Dinwidden. "Why?"

"We got us a twister," said Mr. Cogswell, pointing to the west. Sure enough, still quite a ways away, there was a tornado that appeared to be heading our direction!

We, including Old Jack, followed Mr. Cogswell as he hurried out of the barn, leading us to the root cellar entrance. We quickly made our way down into the cellar while he ran back into his house. Less than a minute later, Mr. Cogswell, along with his wife, came down into the cellar.

He slammed the cellar door shut.

After taking a deep breath, he held out his hand. "Charlie Cogswell. Yes, my brother Curtis sent me a letter a few

days back saying that good friends of his—the Stevens family—was heading out our way. Glad to meet you. And this is my wife Gwenda."

"I'm sorry that we're meeting under such … unusual conditions," said Mrs. Cogswell, "but I am thankful that all of us were able to get into the cellar in time. We'll be safe in here."

"Pa," asked Kate, "will the animals be safe?"

"I don't know, Kate," said Pa. "We can only pray."

"Let's pray that the tornado changes course and doesn't come through our farm or our town," said Mr. Cogswell.

And that's exactly what we prayed.

For the next few minutes, all we heard was the howling of wind and a barrage of raindrops pelting the cellar door. Then we heard a thundering, pounding noise. I can't imagine what being underground beneath a herd of stampeding buffalo would sound like, but that's how it felt.

Then, almost as quickly as it came, the noise dissipated, and soon we were back to the steady pattern of falling raindrops in a blowing wind.

"Well, let's take a look at the damage," said Mr. Cogswell. He didn't sound worried or upset, just very matter-of-fact. He climbed up the steps and opened the door, calling down to the rest of us, "The house is still standing and so is the barn!" The rest of us climbed out of the cellar.

My eyes first noticed that sticks and branches were scattered everywhere. As I looked around, I saw that part of the fence out by the main road was down. Four or five large trees that were part of the windbreak had fallen, but fortunately they hadn't landed on anything. Mr. Cogswell was right. The house and barn were still there.

"I hope you are planning on staying the night," said Mrs. Cogswell.

"We'd be mighty obliged if we could," said Ma.

Pa added, "We'd like to help you repair your fence, wouldn't we, boys?"

And so we all pitched in and began repairing Mr.

Cogswell's fence.

"Mr. Cogswell, are there Indians around here?" Eugene asked. "We haven't seen any real Indians on this whole trip."

"Well son, yes, there are, though mostly they are down south of us, in Kansas and beyond."

"Are they vicious and blood-thirsty?" asked Eugene.

"No, they aren't. The ones I've encountered—you know, the ones who come into town to do business at the general store and what not—are the same as you and me. Now, there is a small handful of Indians who are angry and are not willing to try to get along with the rest of us. They're the ones who make a bad name for all the others. I understand why they're upset—after all, we've settled on what was originally their land—but what's done is done and it can't be undone."

"So we need to be careful?"

"You need to be very careful. If you see an Indian, don't assume he's bad, but keep your eyes open and be alert."

When we finished the work on the fence, we walked back toward the barn. "Grab what you need for tonight and bring it inside the house," said Mr. Cogswell.

"We'll be fine in the barn," said Pa.

"Nonsense," said Mr. Cogswell. "We have room for all of you, if the children don't mind sleeping on the floor. Oh, I should tell you," added Mr. Cogswell, "we've been gettin' some coyotes coming around at night. They're fond of my chickens. If you go outside after dark, keep your eyes open."

"Um, what do you want us to do if we see a coyote while we're walking to the outhouse?" asked Mr. Dinwidden.

"Well, they'll probably leave you alone. They're scared

of people for the most part. But, if one of them decides that you might taste better than chicken, then of course you shoot the varmint," replied Mr. Cogswell.

"Unfortunately," said Mr. Dinwidden, "I've never shot a gun."

"You what?" said Mr. Cogswell in disbelief.

"I have never fired a gun," repeated Mr. Dinwidden.

"Well, let's fix that right now," insisted Mr. Cogswell, putting his arm around Mr. Dinwidden's shoulders. "Wait right here." Mr. Cogswell disappeared into the house, returning about a minute later.

"Gene, I once heard a wise man proclaim that the first rule of a gunfight is: 'You gotta have a gun.' This here is a Colt six-shooter." He pulled out a pistol from inside his coat. Then he reached into a pocket and pulled out a few bullets.

"Here's how you load it," he said, showing Mr. Dinwidden how to insert the bullets, "and here's how you aim and shoot. See that dead leaf on the tree over yonder?" He was pointing to a lone oak leaf maybe thirty feet away. He fired a shot and the leaf snapped off the branch, floating to the ground. He handed the pistol to Mr. Dinwidden and pulled out another from his coat pocket.

"Now, hold your gun like this," said Mr. Cogswell. He readied himself for the next shot with his own pistol.

"Mr. Cogswell, I really don't think this—" began Mr. Dinwidden.

"Gene, you've got to know how to do this if you want to survive in the West. You can do it. Now, hold the pistol like so, and ..."

Mr. Dinwidden's pistol-shooting lesson continued for over an hour, and by the time they were done he was actually getting pretty good at it. He certainly gained confidence in his ability, and when we walked into the house at the end of the afternoon, he was standing about two inches taller than I had ever seen him stand.

23
Hastings

We packed up after breakfast the next morning. Mr. Cogswell's parting words to us were, "Keep your eyes open, especially for Indians." With that, we headed west, aiming for Hastings, Nebraska. Kate, Eugene, and I started off walking with the lead wagon. We were on the lookout for Indians. We looked high and we looked low. We looked left and we looked right. We didn't talk much, as we were quite serious about keeping watch.

A stiff, cool breeze was blowing in our faces, making me teary-eyed. I kept blinking my eyes to combat the wind as we walked, and even though I knew it was important to keep my eyes open and on the lookout, it seemed that the more I tried the harder it was.

"Johnny," said Pa.

I opened my eyes and looked up at him.

"How about you climb in for a while. You look like you're going to keel over at any moment."

I smiled. "Okay, Pa. Sorry, my eyes are tired."

"Kate and Eugene," said Pa, "you climb up too. I appreciate you looking for Indians. I suspect we're safe for a while."

We climbed aboard, and we all huddled together under a shared blanket to stay warm.

I must have drifted off to sleep, but I don't know for how long. I had a dream that I was fishing down at the creek back in Polk City. I was pulling in a big catfish, and Old Jack was sitting next to me on the bank, barking excitedly.

BARK! BARK!

Old Jack's barking woke me up. I rubbed the sleep from my eyes.

"The Indians are attacking!" was the first thought that ran through my head. "Indians!" I shouted, sitting up quickly.

The wagon stopped abruptly, snapping me further awake. I looked around. On the right side of the road was a gentle rise leading to a small hill, wooded with a stand of oaks. On the left side was a ravine leading down to what appeared to be an old, dried-out creek bed. The ravine was peppered with black walnut trees. I looked at Pa. He was staring intently at something to his right, toward the woods.

"No, not Indians, Johnny. Old Jack was just barking at a rabbit that ran across the road. But there's something that puzzles me."

"What is it, Pa?"

"Anyone recognize that horse standing at the edge of the woods?" asked Pa.

Next to the trees stood a beautiful chestnut brown mare with a white spot shaped like a big church bell on her neck.

"Pa, it looks like Mr. Appling's horse!" said Kate.

"Sure does," said Pa.

"What would his horse be doing there?" I asked.

"Well, we don't know for sure that it's his horse," said Pa.

"A lot of horses look like that," Ott said, who had come forward from the rear wagon to see why we had stopped. Elias followed right behind.

"I wonder why the horse is still saddled up?" asked Elias. "That doesn't make sense to me."

"Unless," said Pa, "he ran into trouble. If you don't mind, I think I'll take a look around." Pa handed the reins to Ma and jumped out of the wagon. He had his rifle with him. "Elias, come with me. Bring your gun. You others stay here. We'll be right back."

Pa and Elias crossed the road and walked over toward the horse. I saw Pa bend over and pick something up off the ground. He and Elias talked a bit, and Pa took the horse's reins and tied him to a tree. Then Pa and Elias hurried back to the wagon.

"I found this," said Pa, holding a red handkerchief.

"That's like the one Mr. Appling was wearing!" I said.

"Yes, I believe it is," said Pa.

"Mr. Appling might be in trouble," said Ott.

"Here's what we'll do," said Pa. "Elias, I want you to take Blackie and ride him as fast as you can back to Friend to get the sheriff. The rest of us will wait here."

"Yes sir," said Elias.

"And take your rifle," said Pa.

Elias did as Pa commanded, and in seconds he had untied Blackie from the wagon and he rode off on his way back to Friend.

"John," said Mr. Dinwidden, "I think we should hightail it out of here. We don't know where the outlaws are."

"I know that, Gene, but we can't just wander off when there may be someone who needs our help. Ott, you come with me. George, I'm leaving you in charge of the rest of the party. We are going to do a little exploring in the woods. We'll be back in a few minutes if not sooner."

"John, Ott, you be careful," said Ma.

"We won't take any unnecessary chances," said Pa.

Carrying their guns, Pa and Ott went quietly into the woods and soon were out of sight.

Kate said, "Ma, I'm scared."

"I am too, actually," said Eugene.

"Come on, there's nothing to be afraid of," said George. "I'm here and I've got my gun. I won't let any Indians lay a hand on you."

Not more than five minutes after Pa and Ott left, three men jumped out of the ravine on the other side of the road and menacingly waved their pistols at us.

"Git yer hands up," one of them yelled, "and I mean now!"

Two of these men were the same two men who had tried to rob us in Iowa—Seth and James!

George, still sitting in the third wagon, held his rifle pointed at one of the men, a man with a scar across his chin. I thought back to Mr. Appling's description of the outlaw—Buck Sewell!

Sewell looked at George and said, "There's three of us done got guns, and t'ain't but one of you. Put 'er down."

George realized he was out-numbered, and he lowered his weapon.

"Take his gun, boys," said Sewell. The other two did just that. "Now, what do we have here?" continued Sewell. "Looks like the rooster has left the chicken coop unguarded, and the sly fox has sneaked into the farm yard."

He walked up to the wagon where Ma was sitting. "Where is it?" he asked Ma.

"Where is what?" asked Ma.

"You know what I'm talking about," Sewell retorted.

"If you're talking about money, I'm sorry, we don't have any."

"I'll find it even if I have to tear each wagon apart, board by board," said Sewell.

"Leave us alone, Sewell," I shouted. "You won't get our money, not a penny of it."

"So now, little soldier, you've told me quite a bit," sneered Sewell. "First, you know who I am. That's probably not too good for you, all things considered."

I could have kicked myself for not thinking.

"And second, you've just told me in a round about sort of way that you do have money."

His face wore the most sinister smile I had ever seen.

"Okay, out. I want everybody out of the wagons."

Nobody moved. I think we were all in a state of disbelief that this was really happening to us.

"I said get out. And I mean now!"

Kate, Eugene, and I had been walking. Everybody else slowly climbed out of the wagons.

"Buck," said one of the other two men, "we seen two of them go into the woods toward the hideout, but I thought there was more of 'em than this."

"I don't think so, James," said the other man. "When we tried to rob them before, this was all there was, I think."

"No, 'cause remember, one of 'em shot me."

"I thought that was from the posse that chased us."

"Oh, maybe. I'm not sure."

"Come on, come on boys," said Sewell. "Help me look through the wagons. Start with the chests and other containers."

Still holding his gun, Sewell started with the first wagon. Within a few minutes, every container had been ripped open and the contents of each was strewn onto the road. He had pretty much emptied the wagon, except for the two mattresses.

"T'ain't here," he said, "unless it's in one of them mattresses."

Ma winced ever so slightly, and it didn't go unnoticed by Sewell.

"Aha!" gloated Sewell. "Struck a nerve, did I?"

"You won't get away with this," said Ma.

"We'll see about that," said Sewell. "Now which shall I choose … the top or bottom mattress? Perhaps I should check both."

He set his gun down and sighed, "Why do folks like you make it so difficult for folks like me to earn a livin'?" With his knife, Sewell cut a slit lengthwise down the side of the mattress. He reached in and pulled out a bag. He shook the bag, and it made a metallic, clinking sound.

"Here it is, haha, haha," he laughed, happy as a chicken hawk descending on an unsuspecting fat hen.

He opened the bag and reached in his hand, and he pulled out … a fistful of nails! Angered, he emptied the entire contents of the bag onto the road. It was nothing but nails.

"Don't move," shouted Mr. Dinwidden, stepping forward and pointing a pistol at Buck Sewell. "Now, Sewell, step away from your gun."

Sewell, instead, reached toward his gun.

BANG! Mr. Dinwidden fired a shot into the ground, inches from Sewell's feet.

"I said step away!" he shouted.

"Eugene!" said Mrs. Dinwidden, shocked at what she was seeing. "How do you have a—"

"Drop your pistol," said James. "And I mean now, or your wife is going to get it." James was aiming his gun toward Mrs. Dinwidden.

"As will this one right here," said Seth, pointing his gun at Miss O'Neill.

"If either of you fires, I'm taking this man down," said Mr. Dinwidden, fiercely. His intensity was so out of character that I almost forgot what was happening.

"Oh, Gene," sighed Mrs. Dinwidden, before collapsing to the ground in a heap.

James was distracted just for a moment, but that was enough time for George to whirl around and punch James with his fist. James fell to the ground. George wrestled the gun out of his hand. "Drop your gun, Seth," yelled George. Seth dropped it.

Suddenly, Sewell turned and knocked the pistol out of Mr. Dinwidden's hands. He reached down and picked it up, training it on Mr. Dinwidden.

And at that moment, the pounding of hoofbeats filled the air. Elias and several men from Friend thundered down the road toward the party.

"Stop where you are," shouted Sewell, "or I'll fill this man with lead. I ain't foolin.'"

The approaching men stopped.

"It's okay, it's okay," said Mr. Dinwidden. "Take this man prisoner."

"You're crazy," said Sewell. "I've got a gun pointed at your head."

"I know that," said Mr. Dinwidden, "but I know something that you don't."

"What?"

"The gun has no bullets in it."

Sewell dropped the gun and ran. He reached the edge of the ravine and jumped. His escape attempt was short-lived, though, as two of the men from Friend raced their horses to the edge of the ravine and lassoed Sewell, taking him prisoner.

Meanwhile, James and Seth had taken off in the opposite direction.

"Don't move!" shouted another voice. It was Pa! Pa and Ott walked out of the woods, followed by Mr. Appling! Pa and Ott were brandishing their weapons, and within moments, James and Seth were captured as well and had their hands tied behind their backs.

"Mr. Appling!" I exclaimed. "You're alive!"

"Well, if I'm not, then you are in the middle of quite the disturbing dream. Naw, I'm fine. Nothing that a little rest—and a lot of food—can't fix."

Mrs. Dinwidden's eyes suddenly popped open, and she exclaimed, "I believe the coast is clear!" She stood up and immediately curtsied.

"Honey, you're okay?" asked a surprised Mr. Dinwidden.

"Yes, dear. I'm fine. Just glad I was able to make use of a skill I learned back in my theater days."

"Dorothy, that was all acting?" said Ma. "I'm stunned. That was brilliant!"

Mrs. Dinwidden smiled. "Thank you, Catherine."

"Well, I'll be seein' you," said Mr. Appling.

"What, you're leaving us?" asked Kate.

"Yes ma'am, I'm goin' with the sheriff to testify against these fellers. He said he'll give me some of the credit for helpin' to bring in Buck Sewell, too. Can't beat that."

Mr. Appling turned and looked at Pa. "John, I can't thank you enough for all you've done. I hope our paths cross again, and I hope it's sooner rather than later. Good luck gettin' the rest of the way to Red Cloud. Maybe I'll stop by and visit someday." With that, he and the sheriff and his men left for Friend with the outlaws in tow.

Pa said that he and Ott had gone about half a mile and discovered a cliff overhang on the backside of the hill, where they found Mr. Appling alone, bound, gagged, and tied to a tree. The outlaws had planned to use him for ransom.

Elias, it turned out, didn't have to go all the way back to Friend. Less than a mile from the wagons, Elias encountered the sheriff and his posse. He led the posse back to the wagon train.

"I don't understand, dear," said Ma, "why our money wasn't in the mattress. Where is it?"

Pa smiled. "I figured that if we got robbed on the road, the first mattresses they would check would be in the lead wagon. I put nails in the top mattress. The money is hidden in the bottom mattress in the third wagon."

Pa turned to Mr. Dinwidden. "Gene, I'm curious. Why did you only have one bullet in your gun? It's a six-shooter."

Mr. Dinwidden smiled. "There are five more bullets in it. Dorothy's not the only family member who can act!"

24
Red Cloud

As we began the last day of the journey—March 5, 1878—west to Red Cloud, an aura of reserved euphoria hovered over our little wagon train. There was a feeling of pride for what we were about to accomplish.

Ott broke out into song as we approached Red Cloud that day:

> I'm singin' way too loud
> And I'm standin' really proud
> 'Cause I'm thinkin' about how
> I'm going to Red Cloud, Red Cloud.
>
> Red Cloud — where the corn grows taller
> Red Cloud — where troubles are smaller
> Red Cloud — need help? Just holler
> It's Red Cloud, Red Cloud for me
>
> Not buffaloed nor cowed
> I think you will be wowed
> The land is well endowed
> You'll like it in Red Cloud, Red Cloud

Red Cloud — where the cows are meatier
Red Cloud — where the sheep are bleatier
Red Cloud — where the corn is sweeter
It's Red Cloud, Red Cloud for me

"Meatier I'll accept, but bleatier and sweeter?" laughed Ma.

Ott smiled. "Yeah, I've got to work on that a bit more."

In the back of my mind—probably in the back of most of our minds—there was the issue that once we reached Red Cloud, we still wouldn't be done; we would still have to go find property somewhere to claim. Red Cloud was just going to be a temporary residence for us.

I started paying more attention to what the land looked like. After all, who was to say that some piece of land in front of us wouldn't end up being where we homesteaded?

As we headed southwest of Hastings toward Red Cloud, the land became more barren. We saw an occasional lone tree now and then, but the majority of trees that we saw were clumped together along creeks and streams.

"Pa?"

"Yes, Johnny?"

"There aren't many trees out this way."

"You noticed that too."

"Yes sir. What do they burn for heat? Cow chips?"

"Yes, they burn cow or buffalo chips, but they do other things too. After all, it gets cold out here—maybe even colder than Polk City—and they've got to burn something to keep warm. I've heard that they'll take the long prairie grass and tie it together into a bundle. When it dries, supposedly it burns well. They also ship in coal and burn that. Some people become so desperate for wood to burn in the wintertime that they'll even buy good lumber to burn, if there's nothing else. That's expensive though."

The fact that I had gained a new friend—Eugene—had added excitement and fun on the trip for me. I even taught him how to play soldier, something that Sam Hudson and I used to do all the time back in Polk City. I had thought that every boy knew instinctively how to play soldier, but not Eugene. He didn't have much of an imagination, but soon he caught on, and when I would say things like, "The First Georgia Infantry is attacking," he would point his index finger and start making the necessary shooting noises.

We didn't play soldier, at least not too much, when we were around Pa. He objected to most any mention of the Great Rebellion, so we would play when we were walking in back with the third wagon. For most of the leg from Hastings to Red Cloud, Eugene and I passed the time behind the third wagon by attacking and defeating the entire southern army.

Finally, after twenty-four days of traveling by covered wagon, we entered the town of Red Cloud. Pa followed the directions his sister had mailed him, and that took us to the Cockrall's farm, just past the far edge of town.

It was near dusk when we pulled into the farm yard. The white farmhouse looked to be a bit bigger than our old farmhouse back in Polk City, and there was a large red barn to the right of the house.

The first to greet us was a pair of black dogs about the same size as Old Jack. They were growling at us from the front porch, and it didn't help matters that Old Jack was growling back at them.

Pa handed the reins to Ma and climbed down from the

wagon, and I followed. Pa helped me tie up Old Jack in the wagon to keep him out of trouble.

The black dogs' growling turned into full-fledged barking, not the kind of barking a dog does when he wants your attention, but the kind he does when he's thinking about trying to rip off your leg. Pa usually was good with dogs, but when he tried to show these dogs that we were friendly, they would have none of it.

A slender girl stepped out of the house and stood in front of the door. She yelled, "Lincoln! Grant! Off!" The two black dogs immediately stopped barking and they ran back to the girl, where they lay down at her feet.

I guessed that the girl was about two years younger than me. She had long, curly blond hair. She looked at us and asked, "How may I help you?"

"You must be Susan," said Ma. "I am your Aunt Catherine, from Polk City—"

"And I am your Uncle John," interrupted Pa, "the brother of your mother."

"The brother of my mother? Um … wait just a second, please," she said, stepping back into the house with a slightly baffled look on her face.

"Ma," we heard her shout, "Uncle and Aunt John are here. They said they are your brother's mother." We heard laughter coming from inside the house.

Then we heard a crashing sound that seemed to come from the barn. It sounded as though part of the barn roof had collapsed!

"Heavens!" cried Ma.

Pa made a beeline for the barn, with me right on his tail.

In the barn, we found two young boys sprawled out,

lying on a pile of stacked hay bales. Above them dangled two broken boards, each still attached at one end to the support joists of the floor above.

"Are you okay?" asked Pa, obviously concerned.

Instead of answering right away, the boys looked at each other, said, "Wow!" in unison, and began laughing. They didn't stop laughing for at least a minute.

I could see that Pa was getting more than just a little agitated with the boys. They hadn't answered his question, even though they should have been able to see that Pa was worried.

Finally, the boys got up out of the hay. The taller of the two boys had dark brown hair and looked to be about two years younger than Susan, and the other boy had blond hair and looked maybe another two years younger. The older one said, "My brother and I are fine. We were both up in the hay loft and it somehow collapsed."

"Yeah," said the other, "it kind of just went kaboom!" The two of them started laughing again.

"Lucky for you that you didn't get hurt," said Ma, stepping into the barn. "That wood could have fallen on you."

"It would have served them right," boomed a deep voice behind us. "I had told them not to go up into the loft because it was in dire need of repair."

We all spun around. A man was standing at the barn door.

"Frank!" said Pa. "Good to see you again." Pa and Uncle Frank shook hands.

Ma walked up to him and give him a peck on the cheek. "Hello, Frank. Good to see you. How are you?"

Uncle Frank said, "I see you've met my children."

"Well, they've sort of met me, Father," said Susan, "but

they haven't formally met the boys."

"I'm Samuel," said the older of the boys.

"I'm Micaiah," chimed in the other.

"And I'm Rachel Anne," said a soft voice from outside the barn. Stepping into the doorway was a diminutive woman, maybe five feet tall if she stretched hard on a really hot day. She looked so much like Pa that it was obvious they were brother and sister. Like Pa, she had dark brown hair.

"Sissy!" laughed Pa, reaching out and giving his sister a big hug. "My, don't you look good. I'd like to introduce you to the rest of the family, and to friends who came along with us, but … they are still out with the wagons."

"Unhitch the horses," said Uncle Frank, "and put them in the fenced-in pasture. Plan on staying here tonight."

"Johnny, relay that message to the other wagons," said Pa.

After the horses were taken care of, Eugene and I headed back toward the house and found most of our traveling party gathered by the front porch. We got there before my brothers, who were just a little ways behind us. Uncle Frank looked at Eugene and said, "Well, who's this? Don't tell me—let me guess. You must be George, the big, strong one."

"No sir," said Eugene.

Uncle Frank scratched his chin, thought a moment, and then said, "Well, so you must be Elias, the marksman."

"No sir," repeated Eugene.

Uncle Frank looked confused, but then his eyes lit up and he exclaimed, "Then certainly you are Ott, the funny one."

"I am not Ott," said Eugene. "I'm also not Kate, and

obviously I'm not Johnny. I'm not even a Stevens. I am Eugene Dinwidden, and I belong to Gene and Dorothy Dinwidden, who are standing right behind you." Eugene blushed when he realized that the group had become silent and everyone was listening to him.

"But I'm trying to get him adopted into my family," I said. "By the way, how many steps, Eugene?"

"For today or for the whole trip?"

"The whole trip," I said.

Eugene broke into a big smile and then said, "Uh, I had 2,123,987. And you?"

"I had 2,123,887, less than you."

"You must have taken a shortcut," laughed Eugene.

"Well, after such a long trip, you must be tired. You are all welcome here," began Uncle Frank. "John, what is your plan? I know you are interested in homesteading. Have you found some available land?"

"Frank, we haven't found anything yet, but we've only arrived. Yes, we want to homestead. We want a place of our own, a home that is ours and not something we're renting from someone else. I'm hoping to find a piece of land somewhere around here."

"John, I'm afraid you ain't going to find anything available here in Red Cloud. All the land is claimed. You and your family can stay until you find a place of your own. We have a house—we call it the little house—on the back eighty that you can stay in. It's only a one-room log cabin, but it's in good condition, and it's got a wood floor and a stove that works."

"Frank, that's kind of you, and I thank you. We'll take you up on your offer and use your little house," said Pa. "I will also take a look in Kansas if we can't find anything in Nebraska."

"Kansas?"

"It's a dry state, and that has its advantages," said Pa.

"I understand, John. It's a whole lot easier raisin' a bunch of boys if you don't have to contend with alcohol."

"Amen to that," agreed Pa.

"Problem is," said Uncle Frank, "I've heard that Kansas has run out of homestead land. Everything in Kansas has been claimed."

"Hello, John," boomed a voice from the front door. "Good to see you again." We all looked up to see a barrel-chested giant of a man standing there—he was at least two inches taller than Pa, and Pa himself was considered tall.

The color drained out of Pa's face, lickety-split. Never had I seen Pa look so ashen. The enthusiasm that I had noticed in Pa as we were approaching Red Cloud melted away faster than soft butter on a stack of steaming hot-cakes. Apparently taken aback, Pa didn't say anything. I'm not sure that he could have even if he wanted. The silence was almost deafening.

Ma put her hands around Pa's arm.

I saw Aunt Rachel Anne give Uncle Frank a nervous glance.

Finally, Pa spoke. "William, I … I wasn't expecting to see you … I … I didn't realize you were here."

"I reckon not. I just arrived last week," he drawled.

I was hoping that Pa would walk over and shake the man's hand. Pa didn't move.

There was an uncomfortable silence for a few seconds, and then Aunt Rachel Anne said, "Over in Arkansas, they're having economic problems. Jobs there are a bit hard to come by, so William is going to try his hand at finding work up here."

Something was troubling Pa, but I sure didn't know what it was. There was another stretch of silence. Pa stood there, frozen, like he couldn't think, like he didn't know what to do. It reminded me of an army caught in an ambush, so surprised that they don't know how to fight back. Nobody seemed quite sure what to say.

Ma broke the silence. "Children, I want you to meet Uncle William. He was married to Pa's sister Emma. William, it's so good to see you again."

"The pleasure is mine, Catherine," replied William.

I remembered hearing about Uncle William and Aunt Emma. Aunt Emma had died during childbirth shortly after the war. The baby had died too. Ma and Pa didn't talk about them much.

That night, Miss O'Neill and Mrs. Dinwidden stayed at Uncle Frank's house—Mr. Dinwidden and Eugene slept in the barn, and Uncle William moved out to the barn too so that the ladies could stay in the house—but Pa wanted to go stay at the "little house" on the back eighty, so the rest of us headed over there. It was a one room log cabin, basically a large bedroom with a kitchen attached. We carried in our mattresses from the wagons and got settled in for the evening.

I should have been happy—ecstatic even—because we had finally reached Red Cloud, but inside I knew something was wrong. Something seemed to be casting a shadow on Pa's heart.

I wanted that shadow to go away.

25
A Rebel Flag

The next morning, I woke up to a strange smell. I opened my eyes and saw smoke billowing from the kitchen stove. It was a fire!

I could see Pa frantically trying to scrape something out of the pan on top of the stove. Ma was there too. She said, "John, take the pan outside. There's too much smoke." Pa complied and then came back inside. Ma was smiling. Pa looked frustrated.

"What happened?" I asked.

"Oh," said Pa, exasperated, "I got up early and thought I'd try to surprise you all with pancakes. I used to be able to make pancakes, but I guess I forgot how."

"Your father was distracted and forgot to use lard," explained Ma. "The pancakes stuck to the pan."

"Well, and then I stepped outside and forgot about the pancakes completely," sighed Pa.

"It's okay. There's no harm, just a bit of smoke."

"I don't know, Catherine. Just too many things to think about right now." Pa was frustrated. It wasn't normal to see him like this. Something was still bothering him, and it seemed to have something to do with Uncle William.

After Pa scraped the charred attempt out of the pan,

Ma cooked another batch of pancakes and we sat down at the table to a good, hot breakfast.

"Pa, what happens next?"

"I think we're going to take Miss O'Neill over to McCook right away, probably leaving tomorrow morning. At some point, possibly also tomorrow, the Dinwiddens are going down to Kansas. I'm thinking of sending George and Elias with them for protection and to help them find their way."

"John, do we have to leave so soon for McCook?"

"Catherine, Miss O'Neill wants to get there."

"I know, but I was just hoping we could rest up a bit before leaving."

Pa was adamant though, and after breakfast he laid out maps on the table and worked with Miss O'Neill and the Dinwiddens to get their plans in place. The Dinwiddens did decide that they would leave the next day, headed for Smith Center, Kansas. They weren't going to homestead. Instead, they planned on buying a house in town. Pa and Ma would go with Miss O'Neill, and George and Elias would go with the Dinwiddens, taking extra horses so that they'd have a way to return.

Ott, Kate, and I would stay with Uncle Frank and Aunt Rachel Anne.

"Hey, want to go play?" Samuel and Micaiah asked. Playing sounded like a good idea to me.

"Pa, can I go play with Samuel and Micaiah?"

"Sure son," said Pa quietly, still looking at the maps.

"Yeah!" I exclaimed. I was looking forward to playing with the cousins.

"Do you want to play, too?" they asked Eugene. Eugene looked at his father, who nodded his assent.

Eugene smiled and said, "Thanks, Father."

Samuel and Micaiah led us out to a small storage shed behind the barn, where they wanted to play soldier and the Great Rebellion. Sounded like fun to Eugene and me.

"Okay," Samuel asked, "who wants to be the South and who wants to be the North?"

I whispered to Eugene, "We should be polite by offering to be the South, because they probably want to play on the side of the North like we usually do."

"Right," whispered Eugene in reply. "That sounds great."

"Okay," I said to Samuel and Micaiah, "Eugene and I would be happy being on the South."

A look of disappointment crossed Micaiah's face. He looked at his brother.

"Micaiah, would you rather be on the side of the South?" asked Eugene.

Micaiah nodded.

"Micaiah and I are usually together on the South when we play soldier," said Samuel. "I'm sure he'd be fine playing on the North, though."

"Well, Eugene and I are usually on the North, actually, and we'd be fine with you being the South if you want us to be the North."

"Really?" asked Samuel.

"Really," said Eugene.

"Well, okay, that sounds good."

The battle started and we played for quite a while. Every time one of us "got shot," we were given free passage back to the fort and we could start all over. It was fun. I wish real war would give you second chances the same way that playing soldier did.

Kate and Susan even came out for a while and joined

us, though I have to admit that neither was very good at pretending to be a soldier. They were too dramatic when they were shot.

After we had played for a good while, Samuel said, "Want to see Uncle William's war stuff? There's a box he said we could look at anytime we wanted."

"We sure do!" I said.

Eugene and I followed the cousins to a corner of the barn, where there was a large trunk. Samuel opened it and pulled out his uncle's sword, a couple of military manuals, a gray cap, and a Confederate flag. I had never before seen a Rebel flag in real life.

"Wow, did he capture this?" I asked in admiration.

"What do you mean capture it? You can't capture your own flag, silly."

It finally dawned on me. I don't know why this didn't occur to me earlier. Uncle William—Pa's sister Emma's husband—had been on the side of the South!

My brain thought a whole bunch of thoughts in just a few seconds. Should I be upset that Uncle William had fought on the enemy side? I decided that it didn't really bother me, but it also occurred to me that maybe that had something to do with why Pa was unhappy.

"What unit was he with?" I asked.

"I don't know … what do you mean?" asked Samuel.

"Well … do you know what state he fought with?"

"I think he said Arkansas."

"How long?"

"The whole war, I think."

I whistled.

"What's wrong?" asked Samuel.

"Pa fought for the Union Army. I think some of the

battles he was in—Corinth, Vicksburg, and maybe others—were against armies that included troops from Arkansas. They may have fought against each other."

Samuel's face paled. "So, are they enemies?"

"I don't know," I said. "Maybe."

We had a good-bye celebration that evening. Aunt Rachel Anne baked a cake that we ate for dessert after supper, and then we sang songs around the piano.

Then, each person who was leaving the next day got up to say a few words.

First up to speak was Mrs. Dinwidden. "I must say," she said, bearing a humble countenance, "that I was a fool, a dodo, a self-absorbed dunderhead when we began the journey westward. I'm glad we encountered enough trying circumstances that I had the opportunity to learn how not to be so set in my ways. I hope that as all of you reflect on our travels, you will remember me for how I ended up, not how I began."

Mr. Dinwidden stood up next. "If I don't have the opportunity to fire another gun for the rest of my days, that's fine with me. I'm glad to have had the chance to do something that could help us out though. You all are kind people and have treated us wonderfully, and I thank you. Oh, and come down and visit us in Kansas sometime."

"I don't know what to say, really," began Eugene as he stood up to speak. "I want to say that I'm sorry for the way I acted on the first part of the trip, and I'm happy to have found a great friend—or great friends," he said, looking around the room. "Yes, please come visit. Johnny, come visit." He smiled and I nodded in assent.

Then it was Miss O'Neill's turn.

26
Myriad Buffalo

You know how I enjoy telling a good story," said Miss O'Neill. "Allow me just one more—I promise it won't be long." She cleared her throat and began.

Once upon a time, in a faraway kingdom, there lived a gardener. Now, he wasn't just any gardener. He was the king's gardener. One day, the king handed out little boxes made of wood. One box had the label "Peace" written on it; another box had the label "Joy" etched in the wood. Each of those two boxes was locked, with no key in sight. The third box had the word "Love" written on it. There was no lock on that third box.

Now, the king issued an edict: "Hear ye, hear ye, I desire that my subjects will seek each day to open their boxes."

Well, the gardener tried to open the first two boxes, but he couldn't, because he didn't have a key. He opened the third box, and what he found was a pile of small hearts bearing names.

There was one heart for each person he knew.

The gardener was happy at first. He saw the names of his parents, and he thought, "Of course I love my parents." He saw the name of his brother Ivan, and he thought, "Of course I love my brother Ivan." But then he saw a heart that had written on it the name of his arch enemy, Count Boris. He became angry and slammed the lid to the box shut.

The gardener started hearing from some of his friends that they were finding the keys to open up their other boxes, and that frustrated him, because he couldn't find the key. Each day he would open the Love box and look at the hearts, and each day he would slam it shut when he saw the heart with the name Count Boris written on it.

One day, the king was passing by, and he noticed the gardener. "My friend the gardener, how goes it?"

"Fine, Your Majesty," said the gardener.

"Really? Have you found the keys you need to open all your boxes?"

"Uh, well, not yet, Your Majesty. I'm working diligently on it though," said the gardener.

"Keep trying," said the king. "You'll get it."

Days passed, and the gardener still didn't get it. The days turned to months; the months turned to years. The gardener had put the boxes up in his closet and had nearly forgotten about them.

Then one day, the gardener hired someone to clean his house. The servant worked hard, cleaning every square inch of the gardener's home. After a few hours, the servant appeared, carrying three boxes.

"Mr. Gardener," he said, "you still have your boxes, and two of them haven't been opened. Why is that?"

"Well, I don't rightly know. I haven't figured it out yet," said the gardener.

"It's so simple," said the servant. "All you have to do is open up each of the little hearts, and then you'll find the key."

"Really? It's that simple?"

With glee, the gardener opened up all the hearts—all but one, that is. He didn't open up the heart that said Count Boris. And still he found no key.

"Where is the key?" asked the gardener. "Surely it would have been in one of those hearts."

"You didn't open all of them, sir," replied the boy. "There's one left."

"I can't open that one. I feel no love for that man," said the gardener firmly.

"You feel no love for that man? I beg your pardon, sir, but love is not just a feeling. Love is a decision. If you *decide* to have love, then you *can* have love."

"I don't want to," grumbled the gardener.

"The king didn't ask if you wanted to. He ordered you to."

The gardener thought about that for a few minutes, and then he said, "Count Boris, I decide to love you."

He picked up the heart and opened it. There was a key!

The gardener, quick as lightning, took the key and tried to open the box labeled "Peace." It opened! He then tried the box labeled "Joy." It opened too!

Then the gardener understood. He couldn't decide to have Peace and Joy, but he could decide to have Love. If he decided to have Love, then he could have Peace and Joy. But if he didn't decide to have Love, he could have neither Peace nor Joy."

There was silence for a few moments, and then Ma said, "That was beautiful, Lucille." Everyone nodded in agreement, and I noticed Ma wiping a tear away.

I was sure going to miss Mr. and Mrs. Dinwidden and Miss O'Neill, but I especially was going to miss Eugene. The transformation that had occurred in him—and in our friendship—during the trip was amazing.

The next morning, the departing parties finished loading up their wagons and were ready to head out.

I felt as sad seeing Eugene leave as I did when I left Sam back in Polk City. I guess that's the way it is with friends. Eventually either you move or the friend moves, and it's always hard.

We said our good-byes and I gave Eugene a big handshake. I also handed him a small present, wrapped in a cloth and tied with string. "Eugene, promise me you won't open this until you get to Kansas, okay?"

Eugene smiled and said, "I promise. Thank you, Johnny."

Both Ma and Kate gave Eugene a kiss on the cheek, and he blushed. He didn't complain though.

George and Elias left with the Dinwiddens, and Ma and Pa left with Miss O'Neill. Pa had figured that he and Ma would be gone for about a week.

Pa had told us to help Uncle Frank and Aunt Rachel Anne with chores—and we did— but we also took the opportunity to explore the farm, including the creek down at the bottom. There were signs of spring—crocuses were trying to peek out from the melting snow— and the warmth of the sunshine felt good against the cool, crisp air.

With Pa not there, we played soldier as much as we could. Even without Eugene, I was able to hold my own against Samuel and Micaiah, and the North usually ended up the victor.

The Cockrall children had never played One Old Cat, so we taught it to them. Ott could hit the ball a mile, and we'd keep losing it, sometimes in the snow and sometimes in the fields, but we found it every time. Uncle Frank and Uncle William even came out and played with us a couple of times. Uncle William was pretty good at it. He wasn't much of a hitter, but he was good at pitching.

Down by the creek there was a large pool, and Uncle Frank said the fish liked to settle in there and that it was good fishing in the spring and summer. We tried it a couple times that week, but I guess it was too cold for the fish to be biting much. Kate caught one small bass, but Uncle Frank said it was too small to keep so we let it go.

One morning, Uncle Frank had been out doing some work on a far corner of his farm, and he came back

excited. "Come with me, children. I have something to show you."

We hopped in the wagon and he took us out through the main gate, down the road a stretch, and then he turned onto a road that led around to the back side of the farm. We went up and over a small crest, and there in front of us was a sight to behold. There must have been a thousand buffalo, maybe more, roaming the plains that were laid out before us. As far as the eye could see, the gently rolling hills extended to the horizon, with no roads, no cities, and no people in sight, just myriad buffalo.

"This is God's country," said Uncle Frank. "This is the way it's supposed to be. Isn't that something?"

"Are there buffaloes like this all over Nebraska?" asked Kate.

"No, Kate. Unfortunately, many of the buffalo have been hunted and killed. Large herds like this are rare these days, but once in a while we're lucky enough to see them."

There was a minute or two of silence as we watched the wave of buffalo slowly sweep over the plains. Kate seemed to be in deep thought.

"Uncle Frank?"

"Yes, Kate?"

"When was the last time you saw an elephant on the prairie?"

"An elephant on the prairie?"

"Yes."

"Well … hmph … I don't recall ever having seen an elephant on the prairie," said Uncle Frank.

"That must be part of the reason they are mad."

"The reason who is mad?" asked Uncle Frank.

"The Indians," said Kate. "The Indians must be mad that the elephants are gone."

"Um … maybe. Perhaps you're right, Kate."

"And actually," continued Kate, "they are probably worried that Elephant Bill may get rid of all the buffaloes too."

"Elephant Bill?"

"Yes. You know. His real name is Bill Cody."

"Bill Cody … Elephant Bill," Uncle Frank said under his breath, and then he began laughing.

"Uncle Frank?"

"Yes Kate?"

"Do you think the Indians are mad about that?"

Uncle Frank stopped laughing and his face became serious. "Would you be mad if you were an Indian?"

"I guess so."

"Me too. And I think maybe that's one of the reasons why there are Indian raids happening every once in a while."

"But even if they're mad, they shouldn't hurt people. Pa says we're supposed to love everybody, even if we're on different sides of a fight."

Uncle Frank didn't say anything for a minute or two.

I looked up at him and I saw a tear in his eye. He wiped it away and said, "Your Pa is right. He's sure right."

We left the buffalo herd and took the wagon back to the house. That was the first time I had ever seen that many buffalo out on the prairie. I hoped it wouldn't be the last.

I thought about Pa frequently during the week that he was gone. I wanted to be able to do something to help him, but I realized that I probably couldn't help if I didn't know what the trouble was in the first place.

It wasn't until Pa returned that I found out the cause of it. It had all occurred in Corinth.

27
Corinth

When Ma and Pa returned from McCook—George and Elias returned the same day—Aunt Rachel Anne cooked a feast, including chicken, venison, and fish, and we all ate together in the main house. It was delicious. There was a lot of conversation and laughter around the table, except from Pa, who was cordial enough but who didn't have the same laughter and witty conversation that we usually saw from him. A ghost of some kind was still haunting him.

After dinner, the children helped the women clean up, and when we were finished I found Uncle Frank and Uncle William sitting by the fireplace, talking.

"Where's Pa?" I asked.

"Oh, he went back to the little house," said Uncle Frank. "Said he was worn out and needed some peace and quiet."

I walked to the little house. I had missed Pa when he was in McCook, and I guess I wanted to make sure he was okay.

When I stepped inside, I found Pa sitting in a rocking chair in the dark, facing the fireplace. Pa was slowly rocking back and forth. The fireplace was stone cold.

Without turning around, Pa said, "Sit down, Johnny." I

sat down on the floor, next to Pa.

Pa rocked for a couple of minutes in silence. I had learned that, with adults, the longer the silence before they tell you something, the greater the importance of what they're about to tell you. Under that reasoning, I figured Pa was going to talk about something really important.

"Johnny," said Pa eventually, in a soft voice, "let me tell you about Corinth."

A chill ran up and down my spine, and I could feel the hair bristling on the back of my head. I didn't know what to say and I figured it was best not to say anything.

Pa sat for a few more minutes in silence. He was thinking. Finally, the words started coming out.

"You know why I go to church, Johnny? That is, do you know what got me started going to church?"

"Was it because you love God?"

"I do now, yes. But when I went off to fight in the Great Rebellion, I hadn't been going to a church. I couldn't have cared less about God, truth be told, in those days. I was foolish and just didn't know better."

"Why did you start going to church if you didn't love God?"

"I guess the best way to explain it is that I was afraid. During the war, I saw Hell on earth. The battle at Corinth, Mississippi was the most awful, terrible, sickening, heart-wrenching thing I had ever seen. I figured if there was a place called Hell and if it was truly the worst place imaginable, even worse than Corinth, I wanted to make sure I didn't go there."

He paused for a minute.

"The night before the battle, maybe ten o'clock, I was

standing sentry, watching for any movement out in the woods. We had been there for weeks, just waiting, and every night you could hear the Rebels off in the distance, hollerin', taunting us, and talking. Voices would drift to our camp, and it sounded almost no different than living in town and a neighbor down the street has a big celebration picnic. That's kind of what it was like."

I looked up at Pa. His eyes looked deep in thought.

"But that night it was dead still. No hollerin', no taunting, no talking. The weight of the prayers of thousands of men was hovering in the air, or at least it felt that way. I figured something was up. I also figured they wouldn't attack at night."

"Did they attack that night, Pa?"

"I'll get to that. So I was standing sentry, and I heard footsteps behind me. A voice said softly, 'It's okay, Private—just the brass checking on his troops.'"

I had never heard this before. Who was it?

Pa seemed to have read my mind. "I looked back, expecting to see a lieutenant or colonel."

"What did you see?"

"I saw four stars."

"Four stars! Was it General Halleck?"

"No, Halleck had been called to Washington by then to take over command. It was Grant."

"You talked with General Grant!"

"Yes, Johnny." Pa wore a slight smile, but it was clear that something was heavy on his mind.

Pa continued. "The general put his hand on my shoulder. 'You keepin' those boys in check tonight?' he asked me.

"I told him I was, but that I expected something was

coming because it was so quiet over on the other side. It was different than it had been the other nights. He told me, 'I think so too, Private.'

"The general and I stared ahead in silence for a minute or two, and then he asked, 'When do you think they'll advance?'

"I told him at daybreak for sure, no later. The general looked at me and smiled. 'You know who's over there?'

"'Rebels, sir,' I told the general.

"'General Beauregard himself is the foe. He's a smart man, and he won't do anything predictable. Mark my words, Private, there will be shells flying before daybreak. If I were going to lead the charge, I'd pick middle of the night. Two o'clock? Three o'clock? I don't know. Try to keep them off-guard. Surprise them.'

"'Yes sir,' I replied to the general.

"'Private, are you scared?' he asked me.

"'No sir, General,' I answered. I wanted to show him I was brave.

"'Private, you should be terrified. Oh, maybe not for your own mortality, but for the mass of humanity here tonight. There's a heap of them Rebels, and there's a heap of us. They'll come at us, and we'll go at them. Something is going to give.'

"'Yes sir,' I said.

"'War is a terrible thing, Private. All the killing, all the bloodshed seems senseless at times. But it's not.'

"'It's not, Sir?'

"'It's not. It's for the Cause. Oh, the Rebels are men just like us. They've got families—wives and kids. Most of those soldiers over there are kids themselves. I don't want to kill any of them any worse than they want to kill you or me. We have to, for the Cause.'

"'The Cause, yes sir.'

"'We've got one great nation, Private. This country offers people from around the world a new life, a chance to make things right, a chance to start over. I don't think we can do it as two countries. I think we need to be one—united—set of states. But listen to me gab. I'm preachin' to the choir. Private, when they charge—and they will charge—fight with everything you've got. And as you kill them, I want you to pray for them and their families. But don't back down.'

"'Yes sir. Good night, Sir.'

"'I won't sleep until this battle is done,' he said, and then he walked away.

"My relief came at midnight, and I went to bed. Sure enough, though, at about three o'clock in the morning there was a barrage of cannisters exploding in the trees above us. We jumped up instantly, ready to fight. No yawning, no wondering what it was. We knew. It was amazing to me that with all the explosions around and above us, very few men were hurt by that initial attack. That changed though."

Pa sat in silence for another minute or two before continuing.

"Just before dawn broke, the Rebels charged. They came fast and furious, one after the other in what seemed like an endless assault. They charged first on the left side of the line, and gradually the battle moved to the right. We were on the right end and were the last to join the fray.

"Even with the horrible charge, we seemed to be holding our own. They were falling and we were falling, but we weren't losing ground. Suddenly, though, came the order to fall back."

"Fall back?"

"Yes, retreat. We grumbled a bit, though I think every one of us was glad to be getting out of harm's way.

"So we retreated, and soon I saw why. We were setting up an ambush. Artillery had been set up around the perimeter, and the Rebel charge was running right into the middle of it. Instead of cannon balls, the artillery had been loaded with boxes of musket shot—one box per cannon, a thousand balls in a box.

"We were ordered to stop, turn, and face the coming Rebels. They were just about right on us when the artillery opened up. Hundreds of Rebels were raked down, right there. That whole field of soldiers was pretty much cut down all at—"

Pa's voice broke and he didn't finish that sentence.

I looked up. Pa had his face buried in his hands. I wasn't sure if Pa wanted to be alone or if he wanted to talk about it some more, but I figured the best thing to do was just stay put.

"Most of the Confederate army turned tail and ran," continued Pa, "and we started after them. A few stray Rebels were firing at us, so I went from trench to trench, from hole to hole, trying to stay clear of the bullets. Bodies were strewn everywhere, and a hand reached out and grabbed my leg. I looked down, and it was a fallen Rebel. He couldn't have been older than fifteen.

"'Water,' he whispered. 'Please, I need some water.'

"I bent down to help him—I gave him what little water I had.

"'What's your name?' I asked him.

"'August Satterthwaite,' he said.

"Then he asked, 'Am I ... am I going to die?' He was in pretty bad shape. One shoulder had been ripped to shreds and his stomach had taken a couple of bullets. I told him I didn't know.

"'Could you do me a favor?' the young man gasped. 'Could you send this to my folks ... first chance you get? And could you ... could you add a note and tell them I ... I died an honorable death?' He reached into his pocket and pulled out an envelope.

"I told him that he shouldn't be talking that way, that maybe he would survive and keep going. I don't know why I told him that—it was clear as crystal that he wasn't going to make it. I guess I wanted him to feel better, or maybe I just didn't know what to say.

"Anyway, then August said, 'No, I know I ain't gonna make it. I've been wounded before, and this is different.'

"Then he handed me his letter. The address was written at the bottom. I told him I would send it.

"At that moment, I heard noise close behind me. 'No! Don't shoot him!' shouted August. I turned, and behind me was a Rebel, with his rifle trained right at my head. My rifle was sitting on the edge of the trench where I found August, out of arm's reach. The Rebel's face was darkened from the dirt and smoke of battle, and crimson streaks ran from his forehead down to his neck. I didn't recognize him.

"'Well, look what I found,' said the man with the gun. 'I think I found me a Yank.'

"The voice sounded familiar, but I couldn't quite place it. Voices from the distant past rang in my head.

"'Please, don't shoot him,' said August, again. 'He gave me water.'

"The Rebel looked me in the eye and said, 'I got to.'

"At that moment, I knew the voice. I also knew that I was gone," said Pa. "I had no place to go, no place to turn.

"I stared at him and waited for what seemed an eternity but was probably not even one second. I heard the click and … at the same time, I heard August yell, 'No!'

"August somehow lunged forward, putting himself between the rifle and me. The blast of the gun was echoed by the lurching of August's body. He went down in a heap. He had been killed instantly. August, an enemy, had sacrificed his life for me!"

Pa put his head in his hands. I waited.

Pa continued. "The Rebel who fired the shot didn't stick around to see what was going to happen next. He took off like a bolt of lightning, probably afraid that I was going to shoot before he could reload."

We sat in silence for a few minutes. I tried to think of something to say.

"Pa, it seems that August was going to die anyway. It just happened sooner than it would have." I winced after I said that, wishing I hadn't.

"Oh, I realize that Johnny. I am grateful for what August did for me; in fact, it still amazes me that there are people like him in this world. But … I have a hard time thinking about … the … the Rebel. I haven't been able to forgive him. It's hard to explain."

"Pa, did you read the letter from August before you sent it?"

"I did, Johnny. He was a brave soldier. He told his parents that if he died, he died fighting for the Cause, for states' rights. He also said something else that always stayed with me. He said, live or die, he would rejoice in the Lord. I didn't really understand what he meant until much later.

"I sent the letter, along with a note telling of the boy's bravery. I told how I gave him some water and how we talked—not lifting myself up, but so that they'd know that he died in his right mind. For some reason that was important to me."

"Pa, may I ask you a question?"

"I know what you're going to ask, and you already know the answer."

"Pa, the man who tried to shoot you, was it—"

"Johnny, like I said, you know the answer."

"Sakes alive, Pa, it's no wonder you really don't like Uncle William!"

"Is it that obvious?"

"It couldn't be more obvious, Pa."

I didn't know what else to say. I tried to think of what Pa would say if I was the one who had just told the story to him instead of the other way around.

Pa could sense that I was at a loss for words.

"Johnny, you don't need to say anything. I know this is something that I just need to work through and come to grips with. I guess I've been trying to ignore and forget about it for years, but it's not something that I can stay away from forever. It's time to do something about it."

"What are you going to do?" I asked.

"I don't know yet. I just don't know."

I tossed and turned all night, trying to get to sleep. I kept picturing the battle in my mind: Pa finding a Confederate soldier and helping him, and then Uncle William trying to shoot Pa but hitting one of his own comrades instead.

All of a sudden the war—a nation torn into two parts,

each fighting the other—seemed like a cruel, terrible thing. I vowed that night to never play soldier again.

I was doing chores after breakfast when Kate and Susan—who should have been doing chores—came running across the yard. Kate was chasing Susan. At first I thought they were simply playing, but then Kate tackled Susan and began hitting her.

"Ouch!" yelled Susan. "Leave me alone!"

"Cheater!" shouted Kate. "You aren't playing fair."

"Am too!"

"Are not!"

"Am too!"

"Are not!"

"Children!" Ma said sternly. "First of all, this is not proper behavior from either of you. Second of all, the two of you are cousins—you are family—and if you can't love your relatives, who can you love?"

Pa had been sitting on the porch, quietly watching the whole thing, and he patted his lap and called Kate over. "Sit here a spell, little girl," said Pa. "You and Susan could use a little separation time. You need to cool off and think about things."

Kate sat fidgeting on Pa's lap for about ten minutes, and finally she asked, "Pa, is Susan my neighbor?"

"Well, yes she is," answered Pa.

"So, I'm supposed to love her?"

"Yes, you are."

"But it's hard, Pa. She doesn't play fair."

"Jesus didn't say to love your neighbors who play fair. He said to love your neighbors. Period."

"Okay, Pa. I'll love her because I'm supposed to, because that's the right thing to do."

Kate hopped off Pa's lap. "Can I go play with Susan, Pa?"

"Yes Kate, you may."

Kate bounded off in the direction of the Cockrall's house.

Nobody said anything. Nobody needed to say anything. Pa just sat there, thinking.

28
Surprise

Early the next morning, just as the first rays of light were beginning to peek over the horizon, I heard Pa get up and leave the house. The clip-clop trotting of a horse told me that Pa was headed somewhere.

He wasn't back when we sat down for breakfast.

"Ma, where's Pa?" asked Kate.

"He went out to do some thinking. I'm guessing he'll be gone most of the day."

I spent the bulk of the morning working with Ott. A big tree had fallen down by the creek, and we set about sawing and chopping it up for firewood and stacking it next to the barn. Ott was taking a break, sitting on the ground on the other side of the wood pile while I finished putting an armful of wood onto the stack.

"Hey, look at that," I said. "Here comes Kate, running like her drawers are on fire."

"Johnny ... Johnny, I have to talk to you," she huffed, out of breath. "I might need a doctor. In fact, it might already be too late. Perhaps I'll die before sundown. Promise me, Johnny, that they'll play 'Amazing Grace' at my funeral."

"Kate, Kate, calm down," I urged. "Now, slowly, tell me

what happened."

If you've ever run hard for a long ways and then stopped suddenly and tried to talk, you'll know what I mean when I say that it was impossible for Kate to speak softly, even if she was whispering.

"Johnny, I ... I ... I swallowed a frog!"

I began laughing so hard that I fell to my knees, with tears in my eyes and gasping for air.

Ott started laughing too, and Kate found him sitting on the other side of the wood pile.

"Johnny, you ... you told me no one was around."

"I said nothing of the sort, Kate."

"Well, you should have told me that other people were around."

"I didn't realize it was going to be a private conversation."

"Well, now I'm mad at you."

Ott stood up and put his arm around Kate. "Kate, put yourself in our shoes. If you were stacking wood, and I came up and told you that I had somehow swallowed a frog, I think you would think that it's pretty funny. You'd maybe even laugh harder than we did. So Kate, please forgive us. It's a funny story because, well, it just doesn't happen every day."

"Please don't tell anyone about it," said Kate.

"Kate, Johnny and I solemnly take an oath—don't we, Johnny?—that we will never, ever tell the story about the time that you swallowed the frog, but first we have to know the story so that we can make sure we don't tell it. See what I mean?"

Kate thought about that a moment and then said, "I guess that makes sense, Ott. All right, here's what happened."

Ott and I tried hard, and mostly successfully, to wipe the smiles off of our faces so that we could listen with serious intent.

"I was out by the pond, looking at tadpoles and baby frogs. There are a lot of them right now. I was sitting on a stump for a few minutes, when out of nowhere this little bitty baby green frog jumped onto my lap. He wasn't big at all."

Kate held out a hand with two fingers about a half inch apart, signifying the small frog.

"So ... I've heard all these stories about girls who kiss frogs and the frogs turn into princes. Now, I know that frogs can't really turn into princes, but you never know. It's kind of like making a wish when you blow out the candles on a birthday cake—you don't know for sure if the wish made something happen or if it would have happened anyway. Know what I mean?"

Kate looked at us. I nodded.

"Keep going, Kate," urged Ott.

"I picked the frog up into my hand and put him really close to my mouth. I was wanting to try to kiss it, but I couldn't quite bring myself to do it. I was about ready to set him back down, when suddenly, out of nowhere, I was struck with the biggest yawn I've ever had. There I was, mouth wide open. And for whatever reason, well ... he jumped way into the back of my mouth. I was so surprised that before I knew what was happening, I had swallowed him."

Kate paused and then she added, "I sure hope I never do that again. I could feel him hopping and kicking on his way down."

The image of this was so funny that we started laughing

again.

Kate said, "You promised you won't tell."

"We promise, Kate," said Ott, "and you don't need to worry about dying. I don't think frogs are poisonous. However, I don't know if you'll be able to hide from the others the fact that you ate a frog."

"What do you mean?" asked Kate, worried.

"He means that you might start looking like a frog ... in fact, you might turn into a frog yourself," I said.

"Really?" asked Kate.

"No, not really," said Ott. "You might, though, turn into a princess or a queen. I mean, if *kissing* a person turns a frog into a prince, it only seems logical that *eating* a frog should at least turn a girl into a queen, doesn't it?"

Happily or unhappily for Kate, over the next few hours she didn't show any signs of turning into a frog or a princess or a queen. Someone else, however, changed in a way that I didn't see coming.

29
Tracks

Late that afternoon, we went over to Uncle Frank's house for supper; as we were getting ready to eat, we heard a horse trotting into the yard from the road.

"Pa's back!" Kate shouted, running outside.

A couple of minutes later, Pa and Kate came in together. He didn't say anything, but he walked over and gave Ma a big hug.

Pa looked calm, almost relaxed. He washed up, and then we all sat down together to eat. The table wasn't large enough to seat all of us, so the adults sat at the table and the children sat on the floor.

The thick silence that hovered over the room when we first sat down didn't last long.

"I watched the sunrise this morning," began Pa, "and realized that it was the same sun that came up this morning that also came up that morning many years ago in Corinth."

At the mention of Corinth, Uncle William dropped his fork to the floor. "Pardon me," he mumbled, bending over to pick it up.

"Some things change," continued Pa, "and some things

don't change, and though the Great Rebellion was a long time ago, I remember the events at Corinth as though they happened yesterday."

Uncle William shifted uncomfortably in his chair.

Pa looked up at Uncle William. "William, you and I were both at Corinth."

There was silence in the room. No one was eating. All that could be heard was the sound of the clock ticking on the fireplace mantel.

Uncle William cleared his throat and said softly, "Yes, we were."

"As I was saying," continued Pa, "the sun came up this morning, same as it always does. It comes up no matter what. Yesterday could have been a terrible day, and the sun still came up today. And I realized this morning that the sunrise is kind of like God's love, somehow."

Pa paused to drink a sip of coffee. "Good coffee, Rachel Anne," he said.

Aunt Rachel Anne didn't say anything. She lifted her eyes from her plate and looked up at Pa.

"God loves us," said Pa, "no matter what. Even if we turned from him yesterday, he still loves us today. Of course, he wants us to love him, but even if we don't, he loves us and cares for us. And he wants us to love each other."

There was a pause.

"William, I wasn't going to say this in front of everybody, but—"

"John," interrupted Rachel Anne, "do you want to do this with the children here?"

"Rachel Anne, it's fine." Pa cleared his throat. "William, I've been wrong all these years. I've carried a grudge;

honestly, I've had bad feelings about you for years; but it finally dawned on me this morning that if God loves you, how can I possibly not love you?

"And God revealed to me that I'm not perfect—this will surprise my children, I know." With that, Pa chuckled a moment.

I was sitting there listening to Pa, not sure where he was going with this. I knew, though, that Pa was doing a good thing, a very hard thing. At that moment, I felt like applauding—I didn't, of course—and I felt like giving Pa a big hug. I was proud of him.

"William, please forgive me," said Pa, softly.

William sat there, not responding. I couldn't tell whether he looked confused, relieved, or surprised. Finally, he smiled and said, "Well, I don't quite understand how a God that you can't see—a God that I'm not even sure exists—can make you change your heart like this. But whatever it was that changed your mind about me, I'm glad. I feel like … I feel like we have some lost time to make up somehow."

Pa got out of his chair, and he walked over to Uncle William and held out his hand. Uncle William took his hand and stood up, and the two of them stood there grinning at each other for what seemed like an hour but was probably only a minute.

"Soup's gettin' cold, gentlemen," said Aunt Rachel Anne.

Pa went back to his seat and began eating with gusto. He was also quite talkative. I guess he had a lot of words to catch up on after having been relatively silent since our arrival in Red Cloud.

"Frank, I noticed that part of your fence is down," said Pa.

"Yep, it's from a bad storm we had a few weeks ago. I h'ain't gotten around to fixing it yet."

"Can I fix it for you? I think I'll be able to recruit some pretty good labor around here, don't you reckon?"

"Well John, that would be mighty helpful of you. I'll work with you on that," said Uncle Frank.

"I'm kind of hoping," said Pa, "that maybe while we're repairing a fence together, we can finish tearing down this wall that's been between us over the years. William, will you work with me on this fence?"

"I'd be more than willin', John," replied Uncle William with a smile.

After supper, Kate came up to Pa, gave him a big hug, and said quietly, "I'm proud of you, Pa."

That night, Ma and Pa were sitting in the rocking chairs, and I was lying on the floor next to them, listening. Pa was talking.

> So I rode up past the first few hills in the Republican Valley, Old Jack running by my side. I found a large rock overlooking the river and sat down there to think things over. There was a little bit of snow along the ridge, and the sun glistened on a remnant of snow in the valley below. It should have been peaceful, serene. It wasn't.
>
> My mind was swarming with images from the past, and those thoughts filled my heart with frustration and anger. William had tried to kill me. I kept thinking: *Doesn't he feel bad for what he has done? He doesn't deserve my forgiveness. Why should*

I forgive him?

After an hour or two, I still hadn't calmed down. My heart was racing. I wasn't making any progress on what I had set out to do—finding joy, finding peace—so I thought about heading back. I turned to get Old Jack, but he was gone.

That dog, I muttered to myself. *Where has he gone off to now?* I hadn't been paying any attention to him, so I didn't know where to begin looking.

I whistled for him but there was no response. Then I noticed his paw prints in the snow. I followed his tracks, leading down a ravine and then up to the top of the next hill along the river.

As I passed over the crest of that hill, I could faintly hear Jack barking. I walked a while longer, and eventually I saw him, sitting at the base of a tree on the edge of a clearing and staring up at a raccoon that was sitting in that tree. The coon was not too happy about it.

In the clearing was a little family cemetery, marked by a wooden cross and a gravestone. Carved into the cross was the Scripture reference: Ephesians 4:32. I found that verse in my Bible. You know what it says? It says: "**And be ye kind to one another, tenderhearted, forgiving one another, even as God for Christ's sake hath forgiven you.**"

I read it, and then it struck me. I hadn't forgiven William because I didn't think he deserved it. I was so hurt by what he had done—or what he had tried to do, anyway—that there was no way I would forgive him. But then ... it hit me

that Jesus could say the same thing about me. I
don't deserve his forgiveness. There is nothing I
have done to earn his forgiveness. But he loves
me anyway. He loves me so much that he died
on the cross so that I wouldn't have to.

Pa paused, remaining silent for another minute or two.
Then he said, "If God has forgiven me, then who am I to
have the audacity to say that I won't forgive somebody? It
took me a long time to figure this out, but forgiving William is the right thing to do."

Pa, Uncle Frank, and Uncle William worked hard on
the fence the next morning. My brothers and I worked
too, but Pa really put all his might into that fence. We
came in to eat at noon, and then we went back out to finish the job.

About mid-afternoon, Pa said, "Boys, keep working.
You know what to do. I'm going for a little walk with William and Frank."

Pa and the two uncles walked down the fence row a
ways. We couldn't hear anything being said, but I could
tell that they were all talking. They ended up talking for a
couple of hours, maybe more.

By the time they came back, we had pretty much finished the fence. Uncle Frank examined our work and said
it passed with flying colors.

Pa was smiling the rest of the day, back to being his old
self. Actually, Pa was better than his old self. I don't think
I had ever seen Pa with that sense of peace. It's funny
how forgiveness works, and I don't understand all of it.
I've figured out, though, that sometimes the struggle that

is inside the person who needs to do the forgiving is as strong as the struggle inside the person who did whatever it was that needs forgiving.

At any rate, Pa and Uncle William had restored a long-broken relationship, and the two of them were like brothers after that. God does work in mysterious ways.

30
Up the Republican Valley

Rejuvenated, Pa set out in earnest, determined to establish a homestead. After spending a few days exploring the area, he came to the conclusion that there was nothing available in or around Red Cloud. Pa was disappointed but not devastated, and he wasn't going to give up the search easily. Pa had been convinced that Nebraska was where we were supposed to be.

"I'm going to take a look up the Republican Valley," Pa said one morning.

"The valley?" asked Ma. "I've heard that a lot of the land up in the valley isn't tillable. We won't be able to farm it."

"We may not be able to easily farm it," replied Pa, "but any land is farmable if you work it long enough."

"John, I also don't want to live out in the middle of nowhere, with no neighbors around. I want to have at least some sense of community."

"I know, dear," sighed Pa. "We're starting to run out of options though."

"One option is to turn around and head back," said Ma softly.

"Catherine, we can't do that."

"There's a difference between can't and don't want to,"

said Ma. "Well, go up the valley and take a look. Maybe something will turn up."

"This will most likely be a short trip," said Pa. "Let me take Johnny and Kate. The older boys can stay here to help Uncle Frank with his repairs." We loaded up a wagon and headed into the Republican Valley.

We spent two days going all the way up the valley; we saw acre upon acre of good farmland, but everything was already claimed.

On the third morning of the trip, as we began our way back down the Republican Valley, Kate and I sensed Pa's discouragement, and Kate whispered a quiet prayer: "Lord, please help us find something."

Sometime in the mid-afternoon, we were startled by the sound of racing hoofbeats. Riding fast as blazes, a man was coming down the valley, overtaking us. He pulled his horse to a stop when he reached us.

"Mister … Mister," he said, panting. "There's gonna be Injuns comin' this way sometime soon."

"Indians?" asked Pa. "Have you seen them?"

"Well, no, but everybody up in the valley says they're comin', comin' real soon. They're movin' across the Kansas border and then up into the valley to raid the white settlements. Then they'll move east and take out towns, one by one."

"Has anybody up in the valley seen them?"

"Not recently, no, but they're comin'. We're all sure about that. We just don't know exactly when. I'm sure they'll be comin' real soon." He paused a moment, looked at Pa, and said, "You don't believe me, do you."

Pa said, politely, "I don't doubt that the Indians may be on the move; I also don't doubt that there may be another attack. I think we need to be careful, though, not to panic."

"Mister, it's your hide, not mine. Don't say I didn't warn you!" With that, he kicked his spurs hard into his horse and continued on his way.

As we wound our way back down the valley, we came across an encampment of several wagons. Pa stopped to talk, specifically to find out news of any possible Indian threats. One of the men invited us to stay for dinner and even to camp there for the night. Since it was already late in the day, Pa accepted.

The talk around the campfire that night was filled with anxiety and worry about the Indians. Pa did more listening than talking.

Sitting near the campfire, a man named Charles d'Allemand was with his wife Eva. The two of them had recently moved to Nebraska from Iowa, but now they were in a panic over the Indian threat and didn't feel safe. Mr. d'Allemand lamented that he didn't want to give up his land claim, but his wife desperately wanted to go back to Iowa. She was terrified at the prospect of an Indian attack. It was clear from hearing the two of them talk that they were going to end up back in Iowa, one way or the other.

Pa asked Mr. d'Allemand where his homestead claim was, and if he could look at a map and a survey of the property. Mr. d'Allemand showed him. The claim was in Arapahoe. Mr. d'Allemand said it was gently rolling meadows, with a creek at the bottom, and that there were some big oaks and willows, but not enough trees to get in the way of farming the land. There was no house on the land yet, and Mr. d'Allemand said that he had been planning on constructing a sod house. He also said that the land was suitable for a "dugout," that is, a house that is built into the side of a hill.

Pa asked Mr. d'Allemand what he needed so that he could go back to Iowa, and Mr. d'Allemand replied that he was short one horse, as he required two to pull the wagon. Pa very smartly offered our spare horse—Blackie—in exchange for the man's homestead claim, and Mr. d'Allemand happily accepted the offer immediately.

Before we knew it, we were homesteaders! We were going to live in Arapahoe!

As we began the journey back to Red Cloud the next day, Kate asked, "Pa, how come we're not worried about the Indians if everybody else is?"

"Kate, people get scared about things they don't understand. Yes, there are some bad Indians, just like there are bad white men. Remember those outlaws we encountered near Shenandoah? Just because people have different skin color, or just because people have different beliefs than we do, that doesn't make them bad. They're just different—or maybe we're the ones who are different."

Kate thought about that a while.

"So, no Indians will hurt us?"

"I didn't say that. But I think it's no more likely that we'll be attacked by Indians than we'll be attacked by white outlaws. You never know what's going to happen from day to day. God doesn't want us to worry about that. If you live a life in fear, always worrying about the next scary thing, you can't enjoy life. God wants us to enjoy the life he gave us."

Ma was excited to hear the news when we returned to Uncle Frank's. We finished out the week in Red Cloud, and then we loaded up our wagons and headed to Arapahoe.

Arapahoe! The very name just felt like Nebraska. It somehow reminded me of freedom, of adventure, and of the brave spirit of the American settlers who faced hardships as pioneers to help smooth the way for those who would come later.

When we reached our claim, Ma said, "John, stop the wagon." Pa, with a quizzical look on his face, complied with her request, and Ma jumped out of the wagon. "Come on, children!" she shouted, and she began running across a beautiful meadow. Then she lay down on the ground and began rolling, laughing like a child. "Our land," she cried. "This is our land!"

We had found our home.

31
Arapahoe

The claim was even more picturesque than I had imagined. There were two creeks that flowed into a natural pond that Pa said was about one acre. The pond would be a good water source for the cattle and looked perfect for fishing, too. One stream flowed out of the pond and wound its way through our property and down into our neighbor's property. There were large, rolling meadows, not unlike the one where we saw the herd of buffalo with Uncle Frank. And there was a hillside where we could build our "dugout house," as Mr. d'Allemand had called it.

Over the next few days, Ma and Pa carefully mapped how they wanted our farm to be laid out on the claim— where the crops should be grown; where the dugout house and barn should be situated so that they would get the most sun in the winter and the least sun in the summer; where the gardens should be planted; and where the fences should lie.

After a campfire and supper one night, we were all sitting around the embers, telling stories. Kate told everybody how she had swallowed the frog, and Pa was laughing so hard that I don't think he took a breath for a whole minute.

After that, it was time to begin digging and plowing. On the first day with the shovels, Pa said to Ma, "Catherine, I'll start on the dugout if you want to plant the flowers."

"Flowers?" asked Ma.

"The dahlias and peonies," said Pa.

"What are you talking about, John? I don't have any dahlias or peonies."

Silently, Pa walked over to the kitchen stove—it had not yet been set up for cooking—and opened the oven door. He pulled out a cloth bundle and carried it back to Ma. "Catherine, these are for you." Ma unwrapped the bundle and found … plant roots from her dahlias and peonies brought from Polk City!

Ma wrapped her arms around Pa's neck, and gave him a hug that I thought would never end.

That same morning, a lone figure on a black horse trotted onto the property. It was Uncle William!

"I figured y'all could use another hand building the dugout," he boomed in a jovial voice.

"Could we ever!" agreed Pa.

"Well, I know a thing or two about it," said Uncle William. "Let's get started!"

With gusto, we began digging into the hill where Pa wanted the house. There was a lot of dirt that needed to be moved. It was so hot that afternoon that I unfastened the top buttons of my shirt off while I shoveled. As I dug, one thing I noticed about the Nebraska earth was that there were almost no rocks.

I had only been digging for fifteen minutes or so before

I heard a CLINK! I reached down to see what my shovel had struck, and I found an arrowhead.

"Look at this, Pa."

"Why, it's an arrowhead," said Pa. "Looks like an old one. What do you think, William?"

Uncle William put on his spectacles and looked carefully at the arrowhead. "It certainly is an old one. How old? I don't know. Maybe a hundred years? Two hundred years? Who knows but that this land might be old Indian hunting grounds, or maybe an Indian battle was fought here. We'll never know. Nice find, Johnny."

I put the arrowhead in my pants pocket, and then I dug for a while longer before finding a shady spot where I could sit down to take a break. I looked all around me, enjoying the view, and I saw Kate, lying beneath a wagon, drawing a picture on the slate board.

"Whatcha drawing, Kate?" I yelled.

She looked up. "Nothing, Johnny," she yelled back.

Two or three minutes later, she was by my side, and she asked, "Can I see your arrowhead?"

I handed it to her. "This is really neat," she said, studying it in her hands. Then she looked up at me and gasped, "Johnny, do you feel okay?"

Puzzled, I looked at her and said, "I feel fine. Why?"

"Well, with every minute that passes since you found that arrowhead and put it in your pocket, you look more and more different."

"Do not."

"Do too!"

"What do you mean?"

"Well," she said, "your nose is a little longer, your eyes are a bit darker, your voice is a lot lower, and ... well, I think you need to take a look in the mirror."

I smiled. I thought I knew what to expect.

She handed me the slate board and I took a look. To my surprise, what I saw was a drawing of a buffalo.

Kate giggled and said, "Just don't let Elephant Bill find you!" Still laughing, she got up and ran off, undoubtedly to find another adventure nearby.

Ma walked over to see the arrowhead, and she sat down next to me on the grass. After admiring the artifact sufficiently, she asked, "Johnny, where's your button?"

"Button?"

"The one Sam gave you, the one you wore around your neck."

"Oh, that button. I … uh … I don't have it any more."

"Johnny, did that button end up in Kansas?"

"Yes Ma, I believe it did."

"Good for you, Johnny. I'm proud of you."

"That's okay?"

"Of course it is. I'm curious though. Why did you do it?"

"I don't know, Ma. Well … maybe I do know. Pa told me that sometimes God gives us clear steps to follow when he wants us to do something. My mind was telling me that I would miss the button, but deep down in my heart I knew that giving it to Eugene was the right thing to do. It was as obvious as tracks in the snow. You know what I mean?"

Ma smiled. "You know, Johnny, some of us went through a lot of changes on the long trip out here. I think you've grown up more than you realize."

"Really?"

"Really."

The conversation was interrupted when I heard Pa, working on the wall with Uncle William, burst out in laughter over something Uncle William said.

Some of us went through a lot of changes. Ma's words echoed through my mind. I thought about Eugene and all the changes I saw in him and in our friendship. Eugene's parents, too, seemed to be different people than the couple that started out on the journey.

And I thought about Pa. I had never seen Pa so happy and at peace. When he reconciled with Uncle William, shackles were broken. He was set free from chains that had bound him for so long.

Looking back on the journey across the Great Plains, I could see God's hand at work in all of it. Eugene survived falling through the ice; we had good weather for the most part, especially considering the time of year; Ott wasn't injured when the horses were spooked; and even the wolf attack ... that could have been so much worse. We were blessed by people we met, folks like the Bensons in Shenandoah, Mr. Sawyer at the Missouri River ferry, Mr. Appling on the way to Lincoln, and the Cogswells in Friend. I thought about how God protected us during, not one, but two encounters with outlaws. I thought about Mr. Puffer, the tuba player, and Mr. King, the train guy in Creston, and I wondered if *they* wondered whether we made it to Nebraska. I thought about the two girls on the swing in Milford—Lydia and Chloe, I think, were their names—and the brother and sister in Osceola who pretended they were Indians. Remembering that, I laughed.

What adventures awaited us on the Nebraska plains? I didn't know. But I knew that with God's help and direction, we could all pitch in to tackle whatever came our way. It didn't matter whether we stayed at this claim or at some other claim in some other state. I knew that the tracks in the snow would always lead us home.

Author Notes

This past autumn, my wife and I, along with one of our kids, had the opportunity to fly out to Nebraska and spend time on the old stomping grounds of my great-grandfather, John Stevens Jr. Having grown up on the Great Plains, I felt right at home, not so much from any sense of familiarity but simply because it's in my blood. Part of the fabric that defines who I am includes the dirt, the snow and ice, the intense summer heat, and the various hardships that correspond to being part of the pioneer heritage.

I have never been a farmer, nor have my parents, nor their parents. My great-grandfather (Johnny, in this book), in fact, was an attorney. You might someday read about that in another book. But *his* father (Pa, or John Stevens Sr.) was a farmer, and it was he who, along with his wife (Ma, or Catherine), established the work ethic, moral code, philosophical outlook, and generally congenial framework around which his descendants grew their vines.

This is historical fiction; it follows, then (I think) that part of it is historical and part of it is fiction. The two cannot always be teased apart. In fact, there are several instances in this book where you may find yourself thinking, "It could never have happened that way." Be careful—those are the stories that most likely did happen. I labored to make anything fictional not be outlandish; rather, the fiction helps tie the historical components into (I hope) a smoothly flowing story.

My great-grandfather left many notes detailing events, thoughts, and signs of the times, but he did not arrange them chronologically. He would remember an event; he would write it down. He would remember another event; he would write it down. Never mind which event occurred first, or even if they occurred in the same decade. Mom has been a huge help making sense of some of it, but even she and I have had "discussions" over which event happened first, and where.

Writing this book has been a fun and exciting adventure for me. I wanted to record these stories so that my children and (someday) grandchildren can relive the days of their ancestors, but—for all readers—I wanted to capture what I can of days gone by, a time in the life of this country when the western frontier was shaped and defined.

And yes, there really was a tuba player in Indianola, Iowa named Wales Puffer.

Joel Schnoor
October 1, 2015

Also by Joel Schnoor

I Laid an Egg on Aunt Ruth's Head

Conquering English and ~~It's~~ Its Ruthless Ways

I Laid an Egg on Aunt Ruth's Head: Conquering English and Its Ruthless Ways might be the perfect grammar supplement for teens who already have the basics but could use a little polish. Most adults should also find it useful. Author Joel Schnoor entertains while he instructs through humorous stories of his Great Aunt Ruth.

— Cathy Duffy Reviews

Clever, witty, and surprisingly edifying, *I Laid an Egg on Aunt Ruth's Head* is a can't miss literary treat for true lovers of the English language ... Schnoor's insightful, amusing approach successfully breathes new life into what is typically viewed as a rather mundane subject.

— Apex Reviews

I am not a fan of cute grammar books that seem designed to put down those who make common mistakes. Schnoor's book is definitely not that. He is a kind, considerate, funny teacher who wants only for his students to improve, not to feel bad because of all they don't know.

— Pam Nelson, Raleigh News and Observer

What Others Are Saying About

OFF BALANCE

What do you do when life sends an inexplicable circumstance your way—unexpected doesn't begin to describe it—such as a life-altering, potentially life-shattering diagnosis at 38 years of age with four children and you're the primary breadwinner? You try to connect the dots, because if you can find a context, some purpose, some non-apparent good that can come from what life has sent you, you can find it, if not less painful, at least endurable. …

Joel's is a moving faith journey that goes beyond his own story to give a divine context for all of us who suffer the inexplicable. It gives us hope while we stumble forward to all things new. Thank you, Joel, for helping us connect the dots.

Rev. Ken L. Milliken, Sr. Pastor
Gospel Tabernacle Church, Dunn, NC

Available from www.GennesaretPress.com

CPSIA information can be obtained
at www.ICGtesting.com
Printed in the USA
FFOW03n1212061217
43857084-42834FF

9 780984 554164